Death Wears Yellow Garters

Emily,
Happy (late) Valentine's Day!
Thanks for being my patron.
Rae D. Magdon ♡

Other Books by Rae D. Magdon

Amendyr Series
The Second Sister - Book 1
Wolf's Eyes - Book 2
The Witch's Daughter - Book 3

Rae D. Magdon and Michelle Magly

Dark Horizons Series
Dark Horizons—Book 1
Starless Nights—Book 2

All The Pretty Things

Death Wears Yellow Garters

by

Rae D. Magdon

Desert Palm Press

Death Wears Yellow Garters

Death Wears…Book 1

By **Rae D. Magdon**

©2016 **Rae D. Magdon**

ISBN-10: 1942976003
ISBN-13: 9781942976004

This is a work of fiction - names, characters, places, and incidents are the product of the author's imagination or are used fictitiously. Any resemblance to actual person living or dead, business, events or locales is entirely coincidental. All rights reserved.

No part of this publication may be reproduced, distributed, or transmitted in any form or by any means, including photocopying, recording, or other electronic or mechanical methods, without the prior written permission of the publisher, except in the case of brief quotations embodied in critical reviews and certain other noncommercial uses permitted by copyright law.

For permission requests, write to the publisher at lee@desertpalmpress.com or

Desert Palm Press
1961 Main Street, Suite 220
Watsonville, California 95076
www.desertpalmpress.com

Editor: Mary Hettel
Cover Design: Rachel George (http://www.rachelgeorgeillustration.com/)

Printed in the United States of America
First Edition January 2016

Special thanks to:

Lee, my amazing publisher, for putting this book out into the world.

Mary, my fabulous editor, for making sure it was polished up right.

The generous friend who read through the first drafts to make sure I was doing Jay's heritage and ethnic identity justice. Your comments and reassurances were invaluable, and I'm so proud to be writing about a non-white protagonist.

Sy, for helping me flesh out Jay's character (even if it did require an extra rewrite).

Tory, for his endless support.

Chapter One

JAY STARED AT THE towering colonial mansion in shock. It looked like a giant birthday cake, double-layered and square, with balconies making up the decorative icing around the edges. Tall white columns supported the roof's wide peaks, and the stairs leading up to the front door were large enough for several people to climb them at once. The electronic gate should have been her first clue, but actually seeing the house drove the point home. Her new girlfriend's family was filthy rich.

"Nicky, *this* is your grandfather's house?" She tried to hide the crack in her voice.

"Yes." Nicole bit her lower lip and her expression screamed guilt. "I'm sorry I didn't warn you. I thought about it, but I knew you'd get nervous as soon as you saw the house. I didn't want to scare you off."

Jay tucked her arms tight across her chest. She was slightly offended that Nicole thought so little of her, but she had to admit, she hadn't been expecting this. She had known Nicole was comfortably set. The clues were all there—the hair, the clothes, the way she never looked at price tags. But the house had caught Jay off-guard. She was a planner and she didn't like surprises.

"You should've told me," she muttered. "I would have worn a dress."

Nicole slid a hand through the crook of her elbow. "You hate dresses. Besides, I wanted you to wear the tux. I picked it out, remember? It shows off your shoulders and that tie is so perfect."

Jay sighed. The tux was probably worth more than her monthly paycheck, and she still felt guilty for letting Nicole buy it for her. She tugged at the stiff collar of her shirt, taking in the courtyard. *How many houses even have courtyards these days? Ugh, I can't really blame her for not telling me. I probably would have had an anxiety attack in the car or something. It's way too early in our relationship for her to see me like that.*

Unfortunately, Nicole noticed how jumpy she was. "Stop fidgeting. I think you look great, and Grandpa won't care what you're wearing. He's just excited to meet you. I talk about you a lot, you know."

Jay let out a soft snort. Nicole talked a lot in general, although she had to admit it was endearing.

"So, can we go inside now? I'm freezing in this dress." Nicole clasped Jay's hand before she could protest, dragging her toward the large double doors. "You aren't that scared, are you? You said you weren't scared when we left the apartment. We can turn around and sit in the car for another minute if you want?"

"I'm fine," Jay mumbled. Part of her did want to go back to the car and breathe, but Nicole was already leading her up the steps, marching her to her doom. That, and she had already made them several minutes late by worrying and dragging her feet. "You *promise* this is just a quiet dinner with your family, right? Not some kind of big party?"

Nicole opened the door, not even bothering to ring the bell. "It's just family, but there are a lot of us tonight. Come inside, Jay."

That's me, Jay thought. *A well-trained pet. Heel, Jay. Come, Jay.* That last thought made her blush. She was trying to take their relationship slow, wary of ruining a good thing. It frightened her to admit that even though she and Nicole hadn't been intimate yet, she already felt attached. *Face it, you're whipped, or you wouldn't even be here.*

Remembering that she was supposed to be annoyed, she awkwardly withdrew her hand from Nicole's and followed her into the front hall. The ceiling stretched up and up, supporting a large, dangling chandelier over the entryway. "Just how many people are going to be here? I don't think I can handle any more surprises."

Nicole coaxed her past the large staircase and into a large, lavishly decorated hallway. They passed a few members of the household staff on the way, but aside from a few polite smiles and nods of acknowledgment, they didn't offer any greetings. Jay chewed nervously on the inside of her cheek. She had never been invited to a house that employed cooks and cleaners before. For some reason, their presence made her stomach twist into unpleasant knots. Still, she followed Nicole's lead and smiled back to be polite.

"It's just immediate family, I promise. There's Grandpa, my dad, my stepmother, my brother Harry, my uncles and aunts, my cousins..."

Each listed relative made Jay's chest tighten. She froze in the middle of the hall, and Nicole noticed when her footsteps stopped. Her loose hair swam as she turned back around, dark ringlets falling over the peaches and cream of her bare shoulders. The sight made Jay's heart trip, and it took her a few seconds to remember why she was upset. Even though her girlfriend was a handful, she couldn't deny that just being in Nicole's presence made her happy.

"You are so beautiful...Wait, you tricked me!"

Nicole had the decency to look ashamed. "Well, yes, but I never technically lied to you. It was more of a calculated omission. If I'd told you, would you have come?"

"No," Jay said. *Yes.*

"Yes, you would have, but I knew thinking about it beforehand would make you anxious. I thought this way was best."

Jay sighed. "I hate to admit it, but you're probably right. Better to rip the Band-Aid off." She offered Nicole her arm, resigning herself to her fate. "May I escort you in, Miss Fox?"

"I would be delighted, Miss Venkatesan." Nicole leaned close, lips skimming the side of Jay's cheek as she whispered in her ear. "And I promise to make it up to you later."

The knot in Jay's stomach came back, but for an entirely different reason. She hardly remembered the short walk down the hallway. Her thoughts wavered between the complete strangers she was about to meet and the way Nicole's deep red dress hugged her hips. She couldn't decide whether she was terrified or turned on, but that was a normal state of affairs. Nicole tended to bring out both of those feelings in her most of the time.

She was so distracted that it took her a moment to notice they had entered a wide, spacious sitting room. At least ten pairs of eyes were suddenly fixed on her, and she fought to keep from bolting for the door. Not that she could have broken free anyway. Nicole was gripping her arm tight enough to leave her hand numb. Her heart started to pound, and her breathing sped up under the weight of their stares.

"Nic! You're finally here." A young, dark-haired man in a tuxedo interrupted Jay's panic. He got up from his seat and approached them with open arms, showing a perfect row of straight white teeth as he smiled. Several interrupted conversations resumed, although Jay noticed that most of Nicole's family continued sneaking glances at her.

Nicole returned the man's wide grin. "Harry! You got here before me for a change."

While the two of them chattered to each other, Jay couldn't help but notice their similarities. Like Nicole, Harry had dimples and a mess of dark curls. He was much taller, over six feet, but Nicole carried herself like she was. And, of course, both of them seemed determined to fill every second of silence. She was pulled from her thoughts as Harry turned toward her. "And who's this? The new girlfriend?" She braced herself for a handshake, but Harry pulled her in for a short hug instead. Thankfully, it didn't last long. "Hallo, I'm Harry Fox, Nic's brother. You must be the infamous Jay we've been hearing about."

She pulled back, stunned and a little breathless. At least Harry seemed friendly, if a bit too enthusiastic. "Yup, that's me. Jay Venkatesan. Nice to meet you."

"Wait...Vink-what? Say it again, I don't want to screw it up."

Jay pulled a face. Her last name had caused her no small amount of trouble over the years. "Vain-kah-tay-SUN. But really, don't worry about it. I'm used to people mispronouncing my name."

"So, where are you from?"

"Toronto. Before that, Britain."

"She still says a few words funny," Nicole said. "Ask her to say 'schedule' or 'garage' sometime."

"No, I meant..." Harry paused and shook his head, laughing at himself. "Sorry, that was rude of me, wasn't it?"

Nicole rolled her eyes. "Yup. You ass. But to answer your question, her family's from Southern India."

"An ass, huh? Guess I deserved it. Usually Nicky has worse names for me, but that's nothing unusual for this family."

Family. Oh, right. Jay glanced around the room. Everyone else was still staring at her with varying degrees of interest. "No one told me so many people were going to be here," she whispered.

"Don't worry about them," Harry said. "They're harmless. Well, mostly. If you can handle Nicole, you can definitely handle the rest of us."

Jay glanced over at Nicole. "Your mistake is assuming I can handle her."

Harry let out a loud bark of laughter and clapped her on the shoulder. "Oh, I like you, Jay. My sister's got good taste. Well, I'll let you two lovebirds make the rounds. Aunt Martha and Mum Janine look like they're just dying to see you."

She followed his eyes and noticed two older, well-dressed women in pearls examining her with a mixture of fascination and horror. She looked back at Nicole, pleading for support with her eyes. "Well, don't they look...um." She found it impossible to finish her sentence.

"'Um' is the polite way to say it. Aunt Martha's a busybody. You'll just have to ignore her. Mum Janine's all right though. Now, come on." Nicole stroked her arm, offering her a little comfort before heading toward the table. "I want everyone to meet you. They're going to think you're wonderful, I promise."

Realizing that she was trailing behind like a frightened puppy, Jay gave herself a mental shake and started walking alongside Nicole. With forced assertiveness, she straightened her shoulders and kept her chin level as they approached the two middle-aged ladies.

"Mum Janine, Aunt Martha, it's wonderful to see you," Nicole said, leaning in for hugs and kisses. "I'm so glad you're both here."

Janine opened her mouth to respond, but Aunt Martha managed to butt in first. "I would never miss your grandfather's seventieth birthday party." Like Nicole and Harry, she was a talker, and she possessed the wide mouth to go along with it. Her hair was dyed a rather unflattering color, and her face was suspiciously free of natural wrinkles.

"Aunt Martha, I want you to meet—"

"Of course, I almost had to stay home," Aunt Martha continued, ignoring Nicole's attempts at an introduction.

The sentence was clearly a lead, and Jay leapt on it, eager to talk about anything other than herself. "Oh, were you not feeling well?"

That was all the encouragement Martha needed. "It was dreadful! My Denise had to take me to the hospital. We thought there was something wrong with my heart. My body seems to be falling apart!" Nicole's face turned gloomy. Obviously, Aunt Martha liked talking about her various illnesses a little too much. "I could have died, you see, and the doctor said it was a very serious symptom."

Nicole pretended to smile and nod, but the tight corners of her mouth made it clear that she was barely tolerating her aunt. Meanwhile, Jay studied Nicole's stepmother, trying to interpret her blank expression. If Aunt Martha was a talker like Nicole, Janine was definitely a listener like her. The woman's eyes seemed to take in everything, and Jay squirmed under her gaze. Eventually, she decided to break the stalemate and offer her hand. "Hello, I'm—"

"Jay. Of course. It's nice to have you here."

The words were friendly, but Jay couldn't help feeling that they were a little hollow, too. They shook hands as Aunt Martha continued droning on beside them. For once, Nicole was silent, unable to get a word in edgewise. "And then they took me to the radiology department and the nurse—can you believe he had an earring? What was he trying to look like, a pirate?—he told me I had to take off all my jewelry before I got in the machine."

Janine took pity and ended the one-sided conversation. "Nicole, why don't you and your…Jay, go and wish your grandfather a happy birthday?"

Jay couldn't tell if Nicole's stepmother was trying to get rid of them or stop Aunt Martha from talking, but she was grateful for the chance to escape either way. To her relief, Nicole jumped on the suggestion. "We really should. I'll see you later, Aunt Martha. You can fill Mum Janine in on the details while I'm gone, and she'll tell me all about it later." She bolted around the edge of the table, and Jay followed, unwilling to be left behind.

"You could have warned me," she whispered when she caught up.

"I wasn't the one who asked the question. Why did you have to get Aunt Martha started?"

"I didn't know. I don't know anything about your family because you hardly ever talk about them, and now I'm in a room with a bunch of rich white people I've never met, and they're all staring at me like some kind of freak show, and *shit,* I could really use a Xanax right now."

Nicole stared at her in surprise. "Wow, I think that's the longest sentence you've said since we got here." She grinned and laced their fingers together, giving her hand a soft squeeze. "I'm proud of you, sweetheart."

The endearment and the warmth of Nicole's hand helped slow her hammering heart. She closed her eyes and took a deep breath, and when she opened them, she felt more in control. Nicole had a way of calming her down, even in the most uncomfortable social situations. "Okay, I'm fine now. Where's Grandpa Fox?"

"Right over there." Nicole pointed to a tall, barrel-chested man on the other side of the table. He looked strong and healthy, with wide shoulders and a square chin covered in a smooth gray beard. When he noticed them looking at him, he smiled and opened his arms. Nicole was too much of a lady to run into them, especially in high heels, but Jay could tell she wanted to. Once they were close enough, Nicole let go of her hand and hugged him tight. "Grandpa! Happy birthday."

"My Nicky. You've been away too long."

"I just visited you two weeks ago, Grandpa."

Unsure of herself, Jay kept back a few paces until Nicole's grandfather let her go. Suddenly, she became the focus of his attention. "And I see you convinced Jay to come after all. Wonderful!" He grabbed her hand and pumped it in a strong, friendly shake, but didn't intrude on her personal space. "Nice to meet you, Jay. I'm Stephen Fox, but I'm sure Nicky's told you all about me."

Jay gaped at him in shock. The name was instantly familiar, but it couldn't be. *He isn't. Nicole would have told me...Oh, who am I kidding? No, she wouldn't have. She loves talking about everything except herself.*

Noticing her wide eyes, Mr. Fox let go of her hand. "Well, maybe she hasn't told you."

"You're *the* Stephen Fox? The business investor?" She felt like an idiot for taking so long to put the pieces together. Of course Nicole was related to Stephen Fox. It wasn't exactly a common last name, and it definitely explained the money. In fact, the vague 'nonprofit' Nicole said she worked for was probably the Fox Foundation. Still, Jay was disappointed that Nicole hadn't made it clear before now. For only two months of dating, the lies of omission were starting to add up.

Mr. Fox gave Nicole a disapproving look. "Nicky, you really didn't tell her?"

Nicole shrugged, two spots of pink coloring her pale cheeks. "I know I should have. It's hard enough to find a date without worrying whether it's some creep after your money."

Jay struggled to hide her hurt expression. Even though she knew Nicole wasn't talking about her, the deception still stung. "You didn't trust me enough to tell me?"

"I did. I do. But after a while, it was just easier not to tell you. I knew it would make you nervous. And once I knew it wouldn't make you nervous, I starting worrying you'd think I was weird for not telling you sooner."

Swallowing the lump in her throat, Jay pushed her feelings of betrayal down to deal with later. Aside from this disaster of a party, her relationship with Nicole was good. Great, in fact. The best she'd found in a long time. Nicole knew exactly how to make her laugh, and Jay always felt at home in her presence. That was a rare thing. She was an introvert, and socializing with most people made her at least a little uncomfortable.

Eventually, she took Nicole's hand and smiled. "Mr. Fox, please tell me more about the Fox Foundation. I read in the paper that your board of directors is budgeting more for cancer research this year."

The profoundly grateful look in Nicole's eyes told her she had made the right decision.

Chapter Two

"EXPLAIN IT TO ME again, slower this time," Jay repeated, straining to be heard over the sound of conversation and scraping silverware. She had allowed Nicole to drag her dutifully from relative to relative before they all made their way to the dining room, but she couldn't remember everyone she had spoken with. The last thing she wanted to do was use a wrong name and make an idiot of herself.

"Sure. My grandfather had three children. My father, Uncle Tom, and Aunt Martha. Aunt Martha and her husband Bill have one daughter, Denise. Uncle Tom, he's the one away on a business trip, has two children, Patrick and Tom Junior. And my father has…had three children."

Jay noticed Nicole's correction immediately. There had to be a story there, but now wasn't the time. She decided to gloss over it. "Who's that woman over there, the one next to your stepmother?" She nodded at a large woman who was bursting out of her evening gown, arms wobbling dangerously as she emphasized a point.

"Oh, that's Aunt Beatrice, Uncle Tom's wife. She's had a bit too much to drink, I'm afraid, but that's pretty typical."

Jay tried to look again without staring. On closer inspection, Aunt Beatrice's face was very red, and her fleshy cheeks seemed warm. Her wineglass was also more than half empty, and it probably wasn't her first.

"So, have you forgiven me yet?" Nicole nudged Jay's arm. "I should have prepared you better for tonight. I just didn't want you to run away."

Nicole's soft green eyes made the knot in Jay's chest loosen. She was still a little sore over the deception, but she didn't feel like sulking about it, and Nicole seemed genuinely repentant. "I would never run away. Not from you. I just wish you'd trusted me. All these secrets are starting to hurt my feelings."

"I'm sorry. I wasn't trying to hurt you or make you feel like I didn't trust you." Nicole's warm hand reached out to take hers, and Jay's fork clattered to her plate. Luckily, the noise was lost in the swell of conversation. "I invited you here *because* I trust you. You're the first person I've brought home to meet my family in years."

"You're forgiven," Jay said, her voice shaking. "But no more surprises, okay?"

"No more surprises. Cross my heart." Nicole swept a thumb over her knuckles, causing her face to flush on top of everything else. "Although if you can handle this, I'm sure you can handle anything I throw at you... even Cousin Denise."

Nicole stared across the table, and Jay's eyes followed hers to look at the cousin in question. She was blonde and tan, wearing a dress that scooped much lower than Nicole's. Denise realized she was being looked at and shot them a dazzling smile. Jay was momentarily blinded. *Wow. How does everyone in this family have such great teeth? Guess that explains where some of the Fox family fortune goes...*

"Avoid talking to her if you can," Nicole murmured. "She's kind of an idiot. We all get some of the interest from Grandpa's trust, but she blows hers on brand name clothes, spa days, and surgery."

Jay winced. The idea of cosmetic surgery—breast implants, liposuction, even Botox—made her uncomfortable. It seemed like more pain than it was worth. "Guess she's had more than her teeth fixed up, huh?"

"A lot more. Makes you twitch, doesn't it? I wouldn't be surprised if Grandpa put her part of the inheritance in stocks to keep her from spending it all at once."

"Your grandfather seems nice." Jay picked up her abandoned fork and popped another bite of fish into her mouth. The smoked halibut, at least, was much more pleasant than the company—excluding Mr. Fox and Harry.

"I love Grandpa. He always did fun things with me. Took me out on boats or to the zoo. He never made me do boring stuff like this when I was a kid. He knew I wouldn't appreciate it."

"And now?" Jay teased. "Dating a shy girl who works in a bookstore is pretty boring."

There was a hint of insecurity beneath the joke, and Nicole seemed to sense it. She was quick to offer reassurance. "The last thing you are is boring, and that tux is giving me a lot to appreciate. But you're right, I only dress up like this when I have to. I still like sailing on boats and visiting the zoo better." A smirk played at the edges of her lips. "And going to softball games, of course..."

Jay blushed. "Liar. You only came to that game because your friends dragged you there."

Nicole gave her a wide grin. "I came because upstate New York only has one decent gay bar, and watching the game is a cheaper way to find a date. It was worth it, though. If my friends hadn't convinced me to go, I never would have met you. You looked adorable in your little uniform with your hair all messy under your cap."

Jay shifted awkwardly in her seat. According to her memory, Nicole had spent more time staring at her ass than her hair. When the cute girl in the fourth row had actually come down from the bleachers and asked to buy her a drink after the game, she had almost choked on her gum. "You don't have to keep going to games with me. I know you don't like them."

"You're right. I just like you."

Nicole's flirting helped soothe the last of Jay's hurt feelings. The evening had been awkward to start, but things were getting better. Aunt Martha was seated well away from them, complaining to one of the cousins about her health. Either Tom Junior or Patrick, she couldn't remember which. Mr. Fox looked like he was having a good time with his family around him. Janine still had a strange, almost guarded expression on her face, but the glances she sent in their direction weren't overly hostile. The night was finally starting to look up, and Jay's chest had even stopped hurting.

"Here, Dad's looking at you," Nicole said, tugging on the arm of her tuxedo. "I think he likes you."

"He doesn't seem to dislike me, I guess." Jay had been introduced to Nicole's father, but only briefly. Dinner had been served before they could start a conversation. During their short interaction he hadn't seemed as put-off by her presence as his wife. His main interest seemed to be stock exchanges, and most things that didn't involve money went over his head. Thinking about Nicole's parents, particularly Janine's subtle lack of approval, made Jay feel uncomfortable again. Dinner was drawing to a close, and she wanted a quiet moment to herself. "Hey, is there a bathroom near here? Would it be impolite to get up from the table?"

Nicole smiled. "Aw. I bet you haven't asked permission to leave the table since you were about six. You aren't still nervous, are you? Everyone's been enjoying your company."

Jay shook her head. "Just low-key nervous, not *fuck-I-can't-breathe* nervous. And I still ask my mother before I get up from the table."

"Well, since you're just so well-mannered, go ahead. The lav's kind of far, but you should be able to find it all right."

After a few whispered directions, Jay left the table as discreetly as possible. Unfortunately, finding the bathroom proved to be more challenging than expected. The Fox mansion was huge, and she wished she had paid more attention to Nicole's instructions. Following several wrong turns, she finally chose the correct door. She splashed some water on her face and patted dry with one of the plush hand towels, relieved to be on her own for a few minutes. She appreciated Nicole's boundless energy and constant stream of chatter when they were alone, but dealing with a room full of Foxes had exhausted her.

"It's not so bad," she told her reflection in the mirror. "She must really trust me if she brought me here." That put a smile on her face. Even though Nicole hadn't prepared her for this, it was a clear step forward in their relationship. A step she was eager to take. Everything was out in the open now, and she had managed to keep pretty calm under the circumstances.

Jay lingered in the bathroom for a few more minutes to recuperate before wandering back into the hall. When she couldn't justify hiding any longer, she headed back the way she had come, careful not to get lost again. Her second trip was much shorter, but when she returned to the dining room, she was surprised to find it empty. The table was clear except for a few dishes, and all the chairs were pushed back in. Obviously, the staff had come in to clean up once everyone else had left. "Hello?" she called out softly. "Where did everyone go?"

"They went into the sitting room," said a voice from behind her.

Jay whipped around, barely swallowing a shout. A tall, dark-haired man with a pointed chin was standing in the doorway. His face was clean-shaven, and he looked similar to Nicole and her brother. Jay recognized him as one of the cousins right away. Before she could ask which one, he gave her a slow up and down. "So, you're the one fucking Nicky?" he drawled, still eyeing her as if he could not decide what to make of her.

Jay's eyes narrowed in annoyance. "Don't talk about Nicole like that. Or me."

"No offense meant." His smooth voice implying just the opposite. "I just wanted a look at you. You've given our family quite a stir."

She clenched her fists, nails biting into her palms. "Had a long enough look?"

Nicole's cousin laughed, tossing back his shock of dark hair. "I see why Nicky likes you. In a dress, you would be very striking, I think."

Jay resisted the urge to adjust the coat of her tuxedo. This man's eyes made her skin crawl. He was obviously checking her out, and it made her skin prickle. Still, for Nicole's sake, she decided to try politeness one more time. "This party is important to Nicole. I don't want any trouble. Please show me where the sitting room is, or I'll go find it myself."

Nicole's cousin tsked at her. "Temper, temper. I was only trying to be friendly. Here, I can show you where it is. Nicky's eagerly awaiting your return, I'm sure." He offered his arm, which she refused to take. "No? Oh well. Follow me."

Thankfully, the walk was short. Soon, they entered the same large, cozy sitting room from before. With one last look, her uninvited escort left to bother another relative. She didn't thank him for showing her the way.

To her relief, she didn't have to remain alone for long. Nicole excused herself from a conversation with her grandfather and hurried across the room to greet her. "What was Tom Junior doing with you?" she asked, clearly worried.

Jay wanted to reach down and smooth away the wrinkle above her eyebrows. Her encounter in the hallway had made her very uncomfortable, but seeing Nicole made her feel safe and secure again. "Besides insulting you and hitting on me? He showed me the way here."

"I'm sorry. I waited for you in the dining room, but when you didn't come back, I assumed you found your way here without me. I was just asking if anyone had seen you."

Jay rubbed the back of her neck in embarrassment. "I got lost on the way to the bathroom. Your cousin Tom found me in the dining room. What a creep."

"That was one reason I wanted you in a tux." Nicole reached up to fuss with Jay's collar, and she endured it, secretly enjoying the attention. "I thought he'd be less likely to bother you."

"Really?" She gave Nicole a doubtful look. "That's the only reason?"

"Of course not. I also wanted you in the tux because I think it makes you look sexy. But if it keeps my moron cousin from checking out my woman, even better."

Jay grinned, her cheeks flushing a light pink.

***

The atmosphere of the party improved dramatically as after-dinner drinks were passed through the sitting room. Feeling much mellower, Jay set her glass on top of a coaster and looked over at Nicole. Her girlfriend's cheeks were flushed, and she was even gigglier than usual. "Wow, it's warm in here. Are you feeling warm too, or am I just drunk?"

Jay removed Nicole's glass from her wobbling hand, placing it next to her own on the coffee table. "I think you're just tipsy."

"Oh. Have I ever been drunk in front of you before? I can't remember. Wait. Didn't we go for drinks on our first date? Was I drunk then?"

Jay was a firm believer in drunk-personality readings. Since alcohol stripped away inhibitions, she figured it could expose secret parts of your personality. Fortunately, Nicole seemed to be a happy, harmless drunk instead of a mean or foolish one. "No, I don't think so. Don't worry. It's cute."

Nicole looked almost offended. "I'm not cute," she declared, although she kept her voice at a moderate level. "Especially while drunk." Jay raised her eyebrows. "I'm not!" she insisted, a little louder. "I'm beautiful, sexy, alluring...maybe gorgeous. But I'm not cute."

Jay knew better than to argue the point. She couldn't even win most arguments when Nicole was sober. "This dessert wine is good," she said, reaching for her glass to take another sip. "Oops, that's yours. Got some lipstick on it. Maybe I'll try the port next."

Taking a quick drink from the glass anyway, Jay was about to set it back down when a loud shout came from across the room. Mr. Fox fell out of his chair, gasping as he tried to pick himself up. "I can't breathe! Help, someone, I...I can't...breathe..."

The glass fell out of Jay's hand and onto the floor, spilling wine all over the carpet. She and Nicole didn't notice. They were too busy staring at Mr. Fox, who kept clutching at his chest. "My drink..." he groaned, his face twisted with pain. The entire family gathered around him, but Jay remained a few steps back, frozen with surprise. She had no idea what to do. For some reason, watching Mr. Fox convulse on the floor had left her completely paralyzed.

"Grandpa!" Nicole rushed forward and dropped to the ground first, taking his hands in hers. All traces of her drunkenness had disappeared. "Someone do something. Get hot water, call 9-1-1," she ordered, dodging a swinging fist as Mr. Fox's body began to writhe in her arms.

Aunt Martha started sobbing hysterically, but no one else moved for several seconds. Finally, Harry spoke up. "I'll get water," he said, turning to rush from the room. "Jay, call an ambulance."

The simple, clear direction was enough to get her moving. Jay dug her cell phone out of her pocket with a trembling hand, fumbling over the numbers with her thumb and trying to hold it together. Phone calls were possibly her least favorite thing in the world, and the screams coming from the floor made it a thousand times worse. "Hello? Y...yes, I'm at..." Her voice almost choked off, and she had to cough to clear her throat. "I'm at 565 Rathbone Street. A man is having convulsions...I don't know? He's older, seventy? Please, just hurry and send someone..."

The operator's response was drowned out by another horrific shout. Mr. Fox bent back like a bow before collapsing into another round of wild shivers. His face went rigid, his eyes going wide and round like two white marbles. Suddenly, he went limp and all of his muscles relaxed.

"Water..." he pleaded in a raspy, hoarse voice. "Please...wa...ter..."

"Harry's getting you water, Grandpa," Nicole said, still clutching his hand. "We called 9-1-1. An ambulance is coming. Just hang on."

As suddenly as they had stopped, the spasms started again, throwing the poor man's body to the left as his limbs went rigid. Everyone started shouting at once. Nicole's father and Cousin Patrick joined her on the floor, trying to hold Mr. Fox's body down with their hands, but he shook in their grip.

"No, don't restrain him. It's dangerous."

"But he could hurt himself!"

"Just wait for the ambulance to get here."

After what felt like hours, Harry came back with the water. "What do I do?" he asked, setting the bowl down beside Mr. Fox.

"I don't know. Put a cloth on his chest."

"No, turn him on his side," someone else said. "You're supposed to turn someone having a seizure on their side."

"That's if they're vomiting. He's not vomiting."

The room erupted with more shouts as Mr. Fox bucked against the hands trying to hold him down. He gasped for air through his nose, but his jaw remained locked. At last, he went still. The rest of the group stopped moving, too.

Jay continued staring in a numb state of shock as Nicole checked for a pulse. "I can't feel anything," she sobbed, tearing open her grandfather's shirt and putting her palms directly against his chest. As the wailing of sirens approached the house from outside, she pulled away from his still body. "His heart's stopped. I think...I think Grandpa's dead."

"Wait, lift him up," Harry said. "I see something under his jacket." Nicole helped him turn Mr. Fox onto his side. "Hold on." Carefully, Harry reached under his jacket and pulled out a strip of yellow fabric.

"What is it?" Denise peered over Nicole's hunched back to get a better look while several other relatives gathered behind her.

"It's a garter. A yellow garter."

Chapter Three

"YES, I DIALED 9-1-1," Jay explained for what felt like the hundredth time. Her head ached, and her eyes felt like they wanted to pop whenever she clenched her teeth, but the circle of repetitive questions never seemed to stop. "No one else was doing anything, and my girlfriend kept yelling for someone to call."

The police officer sitting across the table referred to his notes. He was built like a bulldog, the type of guy who had probably been a football player in high school and gone to seed since then. He had introduced himself as Lieutenant Slack, and he was the third person to interview her in the past two hours. The second officer, a thin man named Bellows, was still sitting next to him.

"Your girlfriend," Slack repeated. He tapped his pen against the edge of the table. "Nicole Fox, right? She was the one who invited you to the party."

"My girlfriend, yes." Jay blinked to clear the blurriness from her vision. The past few hours seemed like a horrible dream. Stephen Fox was dead. Nicole was heartbroken. And here she was, being interrogated by police officers when she should have been offering comfort. The only upside was that she was way too tired to keep panicking. Her anxiety had given way to a gray sort of numbness, interspersed with memories of Nicole's pale, tear-streaked face.

"Then what happened?"

She sighed and let the image go. The sooner she answered Slack's questions, the sooner she could leave. She desperately wanted to return to the safety and comfort of her own room, in her own apartment. "After he fell, Nicole got on the floor to help. Everyone else started shouting. Harry told me to call an ambulance while he went for water. That's it."

Lieutenant Slack consulted his notes again, but she caught a glimpse of his deep-set frown. "I thought you said Nicole told you to call 9-1-1?"

Jay sank deeper into her chair. "Yes. No. I mean, both. She screamed for someone to call, and then Harry used my name."

"Right." Slack leaned forward over the table, looking directly into her eyes. "Do you have any idea what happened to Mr. Fox, Miss..."

"Venkatesan," Jay mumbled.

"Right. Miss Vincatissan." She didn't even bother wincing at the terrible pronunciation. "Please answer the question."

"No. Well, maybe. He shouted 'my drink' right before the convulsions started. Won't the autopsy tell you what killed him?"

"You watch too many crime shows," Lieutenant Slack said, but he didn't deny it. "Do you know of any medical conditions Mr. Fox might have had?"

"No medical conditions I know of make someone die like that," Jay whispered. There were no words to describe the violent, horrible way that Nicole's grandfather had passed. "Since he shouted 'my drink' before he started writhing in pain, I assume something got in his system."

"What do you mean?" Slack asked, scribbling something in his notes.

"It's obvious, isn't it? Someone poisoned him."

The lieutenant stopped writing and raised his eyebrows in surprise. The tapping resumed. "How did you get from 'something got in his system' to 'someone poisoned him'? Is there something you haven't told us?"

"It doesn't take a genius to figure it out," Jay said, beginning to tense up. It felt like Slack was accusing her, and the thought made her hands clench and twist in her lap. "He fell over and started screaming. It was horrible. People don't *do* that unless they've been poisoned. Right?"

"We can't confirm the cause of death until the autopsy is finished. It could have been any number of things."

With a heavy groan, Jay removed her glasses, massaging her forehead with steepled fingers. Unfortunately, it did nothing to break up her headache, and the inside of her chest hurt even worse. Lieutenant Slack ignored her, but the other policeman, Officer Bellows, gave her a concerned look. "Would you like a glass of water?"

Jay shook her head. "No thanks. The last thing I want to do right now is drink something."

"I guess you've already made up your mind, all right. Hypothetically, let's say Mr. Fox was poisoned. Who would want to poison him, and why?"

"I don't know. I only met the family tonight. Ask someone else." Jay paused for a moment, gathering her thoughts. "I'm sorry. After everything that's happened, I just want to crawl under the covers and pass out for a year, and Nicole probably feels a hundred times worse."

"I understand." While not exactly sympathetic, Lieutenant Slack didn't seem to blame her for being emotional, either. That was something of a relief. "I just need to ask a few more questions. We want this situation resolved as quickly as possible. After that, you can get some sleep."

"At my apartment, or here?"

"At your apartment. We have no reason to hold anyone here yet."

"Oh, good." Jay slumped forward. She didn't think she could stand an entire night at the police station after what she had witnessed. All she wanted to do was find Nicole and give her the biggest hug she could manage, for both their sakes.

Thankfully, it only took a few minutes for Slack to finish his questioning. He escorted her from the interrogation room, and she breathed a sigh of relief when she saw Nicole waiting for her outside. Her cheeks were dry, but her eyes were still red-rimmed and glistening, and she looked like she was about to start crying again.

"Hey," Jay murmured, opening her arms. She could deal with her own feelings later. Right now, Nicole needed her. "Come here."

For once, Nicole didn't say anything. Instead, she collapsed against Jay's chest, sobbing into her shoulder. Jay held her tight, rubbing a hand up and down between her shoulder blades and whispering into her hair. "It's okay, Nicky. Everything's going to be fine. I promise."

***

A shrill ringing sound pierced Jay's peaceful fog of sleep. She reached out blindly, trying to silence her alarm clock, but her hand only slammed down on the empty nightstand.

"S'your phone, not the clock," a tired voice groaned beside her.

Jay sat up, scrambling to find her glasses. Nicole was lying in bed next to her, tangled up in the sheets. She still wore what remained of her evening clothes, and her mascara was smudged beneath her eyes. Jay winced, certain she looked just as bad in her wrinkled, crookedly buttoned dress shirt and boxers. *Great. This definitely isn't how I wanted us to spend our first night together. So far, today isn't shaping up to be much better than yesterday...*

Yesterday. Everything that had happened came flooding back in excruciating detail, but she could barely even focus on it. The phone was still blaring, and before she could think about anything else, she needed the noise to stop. "Let me get this," she murmured. "I'll be back in a second." She finally traced the obnoxious buzzing to her tuxedo pants, which were crumpled on the other side of the bed, and answered the phone without looking.

"Hello?" she mumbled under her breath, hurrying into the kitchen to keep from bothering Nicole.

"Muthey, have you seen the paper this morning? What am I saying? Of course you have. You always read the paper. That party you were at last night? A wealthy businessman died! You were there, weren't you? Why didn't you call me?"

Jay groaned. She recognized that voice, and she really didn't want to deal with her eccentric aunt Mimi this early in the morning. The woman was hard enough to handle after a solid night's sleep, let alone a few fitful hours after coming home from the police station at two in the morning. "Sorry, Memma. I didn't call you because I was being questioned. Listen, I need to go."

"The morning news says it's a murder!"

That woke her up. She hadn't expected the news to leap to the same morbid conclusions she had, at least not so quickly. "Why do they think it's a murder?" She hadn't shared her suspicions with anyone but Lieutenant Slack, not even Nicole. In the light of day murder did seem a little farfetched. *It could just be my negative thinking. My stupid brain always jumps to the worst possible scenario.*

"Because he was rich, of course," Aunt Mimi said, as if it was the most obvious thing in the world. "It was murder, no doubt about it. Happens all the time."

"No, it doesn't. This is real life, Memma, not one of your detective stories." Although she was fond of Mimi in small doses, her aunt's obsession with murder could be extremely annoying. The woman had enough mystery novels and 'true crime' books to fill an entire library, and half the time, she managed to convince herself that she was starring in her own made-for-TV adaptation.

"I'm coming over right now," Aunt Mimi insisted over her protests. "I want to question you while the memories are still fresh. You should have called me last night!"

"No," Jay repeated, holding the phone with two hands to keep from dropping it. "No, you don't want to come over. You don't need to question me. The police already did that. Memma, you are not involved in this at all. Do you understand? Memma?" But Aunt Mimi had already hung up. Jay set her phone on the kitchen island, hanging her head and resigning herself to her fate. There would be no escape now.

***

The doorbell rang a few minutes later, just as Jay was pulling on a fresh pair of jeans. She turned to look at the bed, waiting silently to see if the sound would wake her sleeping guest. Fortunately, Nicole's eyes remained shut as she cuddled closer to one of the pillows. "Please stay asleep," Jay murmured, reaching down to tuck aside a lock of Nicole's dark hair. "At least until I get rid of Aunt Mimi. God knows what crazy things she'd say if she met you."

After placing a soft kiss on Nicole's forehead, she headed for the front door. She stumbled through the hallway barefoot, struggling to button her pants and pull up her zipper at the same time. At last, she reached the door, mostly dressed, but still nervous. "Memma?" she called, looking out through the peephole. "Are you there?"

A large, distorted pair of eyes greeted her as Aunt Mimi peered back in through the other end. "Well, don't just leave me standing out here. Let me in."

There was no other choice. Aunt Mimi was as stubborn as she was nosey, and Jay knew she wouldn't leave without answers. Reluctantly, Jay opened the door and stepped aside. Aunt Mimi burst into the apartment, clutching a bright yellow purse close to her full chest. Her colorful purses were a staple of her outfits, along with the matching shoes.

"You look awful." Aunt Mimi frowned in disapproval. "Didn't you get any sleep at all? Wait, have you been taking your medication?"

"No, and not yet." With a sigh, Jay trudged into the kitchen to prepare coffee. It probably wasn't the greatest idea with how jittery and exhausted she was feeling, but she would need it to deal with Aunt Mimi's crazy detective theories at seven in the morning. "I haven't even had time to take a shower."

"I suppose that's to be expected. Someone did die last night. Now, about the murder—"

"There was no murder." Jay continued filling the coffee pot with water as Aunt Mimi sat down at the kitchen table. She forced herself to forget that she had thought it was a murder the night before as she spooned the coffee into the filter. If Aunt Mimi was going to believe the worst possible scenario too, she wanted no part in it. Even she wasn't that crazy. "He could have had a seizure or maybe a heart attack."

"A heart attack? Not a chance." Aunt Mimi removed a pen from the depths of her purse and shoved it between her teeth, speaking around it as she continued rummaging for something else. "Of coursh it wash a murdeh." She spat out the pen and made a satisfied noise as she located a small pad of notebook paper. "Now, you have to tell me all about this little party. I need all the details, even things you don't think are important."

Jay switched on the coffee pot and leaned back against the counter, folding her arms over her chest. The more insistent Mimi was, the more determined Jay became to convince her otherwise. The last thing she needed was her crazy aunt running around and screaming murder on top of everything else. "The police are already looking into it. No matter what happened, I'm sure they'll figure it out." She gave Aunt Mimi a pleading look. "Please, just let them do their job. This isn't one of your books."

The determination on Aunt Mimi's face didn't waver. "We'll see about that."

Jay knew a lost cause when she saw one. Nothing would dissuade Mimi from interrogating someone about Stephen Fox's death. *Well, if she's going to question somebody, it might as well be me. I don't want her bothering Nicole the morning after her grandfather died or heading down to pester Lieutenant Slack and getting herself arrested. And she* would *do both of those things.*

"Fine, Memma. If I let you 'interview' me, will you go away?" Before Aunt Mimi could promise, Jay poured two cups of coffee and plopped down in the seat next to her. "Okay, it's a deal. I'll tell you what I remember..."

Half an hour later, Aunt Mimi still wasn't satisfied with her explanation. "A yellow garter? Are you sure? Were any of the ladies at the party wearing yellow?" Jay tried to remember, taking a sip of her coffee to stall for time. Aunt Mimi slapped her hand away and retrieved the mug. "That's mine, not yours."

"Sorry, I'm tired. And no, I don't think anyone was wearing yellow. Besides, it was an old fashioned garter. It's not the kind of thing you'd wear to a dinner party."

"Just what I was thinking. That leaves only one possible

explanation. The murderer dropped it as a clue to their identity."

"I'm still not sure it was a murder," Jay lied, willing to fudge her own opinions to keep Aunt Mimi from getting too excited. "Murderers are too smart to drop stuff at the scene of a crime."

As usual, Aunt Mimi refused to be dissuaded. "It's not a matter of stupidity. They must have done it on purpose."

"You keep saying 'they' instead of 'he'. Do you think the murderer is a she?"

"Possibly. Poison does have a feminine touch. Do you know how many women have killed off their husbands with arsenic?"

"No, but I'm sure you're going to tell me."

"A lot, that's how many!" Aunt Mimi's horn-rimmed glasses went askew on her nose, and she had to calm down for a moment to push them back into place. She leaned close, staring deep into Jay's eyes. "I'm afraid there's no question. It was murder. Cruel, cold-blooded murder."

A soft gasp came from behind them, and Jay whirled around in her chair. Nicole was standing at the edge of the kitchen, swallowed up in one of her spare T-shirts. Although last night's smeared makeup had been washed from her face, she didn't look much better. Her skin was unnaturally pale, and there were grief lines around her eyes. "Jay?" she asked in a shaking voice. "Who is this?

Jay set her mug aside and left the table, hurrying over to Nicole. She ran a comforting hand along Nicole's arm, staring at her with a mixture of concern and embarrassment. "You should go back to bed, Nicky. This is just Memma...I mean, my Aunt Mimi. She was about to leave."

Nicole ignored the suggestion, circling around her and heading for the table. She approached Aunt Mimi and sat down in one of the empty chairs, wiping her red eyes even though she wasn't crying. "Do you really think it was a murder? Why would someone want to kill my grandpa? It was...horrible..."

"No one knows what happened to your grandfather yet," Jay said. She rested her hands on the back of Nicole's chair, glaring at Mimi and warning her to stay silent. "They haven't done the autopsy. It might have been a medical issue or an accident."

"What kind of accident is it when someone takes a sip of their drink and ends up on the floor dead?" Nicole turned around, staring up at her with hard, determined eyes. "If this was a murder, I want the killer found. Even if it's a member of my own family."

"It must be a member of your family," Aunt Mimi said, unable to hide the edge of excitement in her voice. "No one else there had a clear motive for murder." A strange light came to her eyes, one that made Jay want to hide her face in her hands.

"Don't encourage her," Jay said, unsure whether she was talking to Nicole or Aunt Mimi. "None of us should make assumptions about what happened."

"We're not making assumptions. We're making educated guesses. Aren't we, my dear? Jay, can't you find something for Nicole to wear besides an old shirt? Go get her some proper clothes."

Nicole blushed, tugging at the hem of her T-shirt. "Most of Jay's clothes don't fit me. We aren't the same size..." Her voice trailed off, and she studied Aunt Mimi with renewed interest. "I'm sorry, I never introduced myself. I'm Nicole Fox." She held out her hand and Aunt Mimi shook it.

"I know, dear. Jay's told me a lot about you. I'm sorry my niece was rude enough to forget introductions."

Jay took the blame in silence, not wanting to aggravate either of her guests. "Listen," she pleaded instead, desperate for a change of subject. "Nicole and I have to get back to the police station this morning. Why don't we go out to breakfast first? My fridge is empty." It was a long shot, but she secretly hoped Aunt Mimi would be less likely to interrogate Nicole while she was stuffing her face with food.

Aunt Mimi gave her a terrifying smile. "That's a wonderful idea, muthey. Go find Nicole something else to wear, and we can all get breakfast. I need to question her anyway."

"No, you don't need to question anyone," Jay protested, but Nicole and Aunt Mimi were already lost in their own conversation. With a sigh, she wandered back to the bedroom to hunt for some smaller clothes.

Chapter Four

JAY TRUDGED ACROSS THE police station parking lot at Nicole's side, shoving her hands in her pockets for warmth. Breakfast with Aunt Mimi had been about what she expected—a fast-paced barrage of questions and wild accusations. Fortunately, or perhaps unfortunately, Nicole seemed interested in Mimi's theories instead of offended by them. Although a few shadows had crept across her face, the thought of finding the person responsible for killing her grandfather seemed to cheer Nicole up.

"I'm really sorry about her," Jay said as they made their way up the walk, the same refrain she had been repeating for the past hour.

Nicole turned to look at her, breath curling up in silver streams of smoke. "You don't have to keep apologizing. Your Aunt Mimi just said what both of us were thinking. At least she wants to do something about it, you know? Even if it's not really any of her business."

"It doesn't matter. She shouldn't have been bothering you like that. You just lost your grandfather."

Nicole's eyes glistened for a moment, but she blinked them clear. She reached out, and Jay took her icy hand, trying to rub some warmth into it. "Yes, I did. But I can't live with the thought that someone in my family might have killed him. Your Aunt Mimi is right. Whoever it is, I want them caught."

Jay nodded silently and led Nicole into the police station, heading straight for the front desk. After signing in, they were taken to separate rooms. Her heart lurched as Bellows, the young officer from the night before, led Nicole to the other end of the hall. Part of her didn't want to say goodbye. Awful thoughts kept flashing in her mind—Nicole collapsing to the floor instead of her grandfather, face twisted in agony.

She sucked on her teeth, burying the images deep down and trying to remember what her therapist had told her. *This is my anxiety talking. Just because something bad* might *happen doesn't mean it will happen for sure. The probability is vanishingly small...* But that vanishingly small probability hadn't stopped Nicole's grandfather from dying a horrible death.

"Miss Vincatissin?" someone called, snapping her from her thoughts. She looked up to see Lieutenant Slack waiting a few yards away. "We're ready for you in room three." She stood up and followed him without a word, passing through the door as he held it open.

Soon, she and Slack were seated across from each other once again. He looked tired, and she wondered how late he had stayed up compiling information. His stack of papers had doubled in size since the previous night. "Between all the reports, we have a pretty good picture of what was happening in the room when Mr. Fox's convulsions started. Now, I want to know more about his family. An outside perspective."

Jay took the lead half-heartedly. "I can't tell you much. Before last night, I didn't even know Nicole was Stephen Fox's granddaughter."

"Did he know about you?"

"I think so. He knew my name, and he was nice to me. I guess Nicole talked about me before the party." Thinking about Mr. Fox's kind acceptance made a lump form in her throat. Even though she had only known him for a few hours, she felt sick thinking about what had happened to him.

"And the rest of the Foxes? Did they like you?"

She hunched her shoulders. "Does it matter?"

"Yeah, it does."

Jay sighed. "Nicole's stepmother was a little cold, but polite. Her father and I got along okay. Aunt Martha was put off when I first came in, but once she was the center of attention again, she stopped caring. The other aunts and uncles pretty much ignored me."

"What about the younger crowd? There were lots of grandchildren at the party, right?"

"Yeah. Harry really seemed to like me. Denise just talked about clothes, mostly, and Patrick blended into the wallpaper. Tom Junior tried to hit on me, but I told him to shove it. Things calmed down by the time we started drinking in the sitting room. Until...you know." She stared down at her lap, toes jumping inside her shoes. Her chest was starting to hurt again. Hopefully, this interview wouldn't last as long as the others.

Lieutenant Slack ignored her fidgeting. "So, you didn't think any family members were acting hostile toward Mr. Fox?"

"No. Wait, are you treating this as a homicide case?" Lieutenant

Slack started to protest, but she held up a hand. She didn't normally interrupt other people, preferring to listen rather than talk, but she didn't want to lose her nerve. "Hold on, I've got a reason for asking. I have this crazy Aunt Mimi, right? And she likes to read mystery novels and watch detective shows. She thinks she's some kind of modern day Miss Marple, I guess, because she's decided she wants to solve this case. Or something."

She wasn't surprised when Lieutenant Slack gave her an odd look. The explanation sounded ridiculous even to her own ears.

"Let me try again," she stammered, her face hot with embarrassment. "My Aunt Mimi...well...if a middle-aged woman with a crazy handbag and matching shoes ever comes snooping around, don't freak out. She's harmless. Mostly. Call me if she bothers you while you're investigating, and I'll come get her."

Lieutenant Slack snorted with what could have been laughter. Jay didn't blame him. The whole thing did seem crazy when she spelled it out. "If your aunt Mimi does show up, I'll be sure to notify you, but we'll have to step in if she causes trouble for the investigation."

"She won't cause any trouble," Jay said, although her voice didn't hold much confidence. "I promise."

Before Slack could respond, there was a knock on the door. "Come in," he barked, and the door opened to reveal Bellows shifting from foot to foot.

"Loo? Chief's on the phone for you. He doesn't sound happy."

Slack shook his head, picking himself up out of his chair with a grunt. "Of course he isn't. He's probably got the Mayor breathing down his neck already."

Jay felt a small wave of sympathy for him. Judging by the look on his face, Mr. Fox's murder was causing him no small amount of stress. She could relate. She had been in a constant state of stress ever since she first laid eyes on the Fox family mansion.

"He wants names," Bellows said. "Told me to tell you he wants to know who poisoned the poor bastard, and he wants to know now."

Slack aimed a disapproving glare in his direction. "Bellows, you'll never make detective if you refer to the victims as 'poor bastards.'"

Bellows rubbed the back of his neck in embarrassment. "I was just repeating what the chief said, sir."

"Yeah," Slack snorted. "In front of a suspect."

Jay's eyes widened. "I'm a *suspect*?" She choked a little on the word, but it had already rattled her. Her breathing went shallow, and she dug her fingers into her knees, trying to ignore the painful knot stuck behind her ribs.

"Technically." If Slack noticed her distress, he didn't let on. "But I'll be honest with you. I don't think you did it. You're at the very bottom of my list."

"But you have a guess, don't you?" Bellows interrupted.

Slack sighed. He moved a pinched forefinger and thumb to his lips, mimicking the motion of smoking a cigarette.

"I have too many guesses. Everyone stood to benefit from Stephen Fox's death. Everyone except Miss Vinkatessun here has a motive."

"You sound like my aunt Mimi," Jay muttered. Her voice was a dull wash, but her heart sounded unnaturally loud as it thudded in her ears. "Only without the crazy."

Slack bent down to scoop up his paperwork from the table. "You can go back to the waiting room now. I'll give you a call if that aunt of yours shows up. Hopefully, we won't have any problems."

"I hope so, too." But somehow, she doubted it.

***

Jay's heart sank when she realized Nicole wasn't waiting for her at the front of the station. After gazing hopefully around the room and giving the receptionist an awkward smile, she plopped down in one of the uncomfortable chairs by the window. She rested her forehead against the cool glass, staring out at the parking lot.

The images came flooding back. *Nicole, writhing on the ground, eyes glazed with pain...* She blinked and noticed her breath fogging up the corner of the window. Impulsively, she traced a face in the middle of the blurry patch, dotting its eyes and giving it a wide grin. *Nicole, reaching out toward her with a jerking hand...*

She breathed on the glass again and drew a heart with the tip of her finger. After a moment of hesitation, she added 'J + N' in the middle. The childish gesture made her feel a little better. Just as she finished, someone came up behind her and cleared their throat. "So they finally let you escape too, huh? Have you seen my sister yet?"

Jay turned around to see Harry standing in front of her chair. She wiped the window clear with her sleeve, avoiding his eyes. "I drove her here this morning. She was really upset last night, so I let her sleep with me." She blushed and immediately tried to correct herself. "I meant we both just went right to sleep."

Harry laughed. "I know what you meant, Vinnie." Jay gave him a confused look. "Look, no offense, but your last name's impossible to say. I've decided Vinnie is my new nickname for you."

"You could always use my first name," she suggested quietly, but Harry just kept grinning at her.

"No chance. Where's the fun in that?"

"Who's having fun?" another voice asked. Jay's frown turned into a smile when she saw Nicole exiting the hallway. "You're not bothering my girlfriend, are you, Harry? Please don't run this one off. I really like her." Although she was trying to look cheerful, Jay could tell Nicole was tired. Her eyes were glazed over and her shoulders were slumped with exhaustion.

Harry gave her a wounded look. "Me? Never. So, what did the police question you about?"

"We aren't supposed to talk about the investigation." Nicole headed for the door, dragging him by his sleeve. Jay stood and followed them out into the crisp winter air, pulling the collar of her jacket up around her face.

"Are you really not going to tell me?" Harry asked as they stepped out into the parking lot.

"No, I will. I just wanted to get out of there." Nicole surprised Jay by reaching for her hand. It wasn't cold enough for mittens yet, and the warmth around her fingers felt nice. "They mostly questioned me about Grandpa's will. They wanted to know where all his money went if he died, and if he had an insurance policy. That kind of thing."

"Looking for a motive, I guess. Did you tell them?"

"I told them what I knew. The physical property goes to our dad, Aunt Martha, and Uncle Tom. We all get a share of the trust's interest."

"You should have told them to get a judge's order and go to our lawyers. That kind of thing is confidential."

"I didn't realize it was a big secret," Nicole said, a little defensively. "Why does it matter?"

"I suppose it doesn't. My car is on the other side of the lot. I'll see you soon, sis. Vinnie, you too. Try to keep Nic out of trouble. Actually, get her into some. It might be good for her."

Jay watched Harry walk away, shaking her head in disbelief. "I know," Nicole said. "He's too much, isn't he? Where are your keys? I'll drive. I want to be in control of something in my goddamn life for a few minutes." Before she could answer, Nicole's hand slid into her back pocket, pulling out her keys and groping her ass along the way. Jay squeaked in surprise, but Nicole didn't seem to notice. "So, what did the police question you about?"

Jay shrugged as she walked around to the passenger's side. "Your family, mostly. Lieutenant Slack asked if anyone was threatening your grandpa. I said no." Her voice trailed off, and they sat in uncomfortable silence as she waited for Nicole to pull out of the lot.

Nicole reached over to squeeze her thigh. "It's okay, Jay. I'm okay. You don't have to keep worrying about me."

The soft touch made Jay's stomach tie itself in knots. She turned in her seat, looking at Nicole with concerned eyes. "Are you kidding? I'm always worried anyway. I might as well worry about something worthwhile, like you." Smooth, warm fingers reached up to stroke her cheek, and the sight of Nicole's rosebud mouth smiling up at her made her heart thump against the cage of her ribs. *Shit. I am so gone.*

"You know, some people would have cut and run during this mess," Nicole said. "But I'm glad you didn't."

"I could never run." *Then you would never look at me like this again. Like you want me.* It was too soon to say 'I love you', but she couldn't help thinking something like it. She inched closer, watching Nicole's face for any sign of uncertainty. To her relief, Nicole leaned forward as well. It was hard to tell who made contact first, but when their lips met, Jay smiled into the kiss. The mouth beneath hers was warm, sweet, and familiar. Exactly what she needed. She wanted to linger there as long as possible.

She kept her eyes closed at first, but when she finally peeked, she noticed Nicole staring, too. They both broke apart and started laughing. *It feels good to laugh*, she thought as Nicole's forehead dipped to rest on her shoulder. It was a nice change from the past several hours. It was also nice to be with Nicole. Nicole, who was alive with slow, steady breaths and soft lips. Her fears retreated to a dark corner in the back of her mind.

"Hey," Nicole murmured, patting her knee as she shifted back into her own seat. "I'm not ready to go home by myself. Can we head back to your place for a little while? Maybe watch a movie?"

"Sure. I'd like that." *I'm not ready to let you go yet.*

Nicole gave her a grateful look. "Thanks. For everything. You've been perfect during all of this. I don't know how I would have coped without you."

"You would've been fine," Jay said, but the compliment made her chest swell. "So, what movie do you want to watch?"

Nicole put the car in drive and pulled out of the parking space. "It doesn't matter. I'm planning on making out with you during most of it."

Jay's eyes widened in surprise. "Are you sure? I...I didn't think...I mean, you don't have to..."

"It's what Grandpa would have wanted." A small smile crossed Nicole's face when Jay started sputtering. "Don't look at me like that. He was a pretty enlightened guy. I came out to him before either of my parents. And even though he was devoted to his work, he always took time to enjoy life and be with the people he cared about. I want to be just like him."

Although she tried not to read too much into the comment, Jay couldn't help grinning. Even though everything else seemed to be going wrong all at once, her budding relationship with Nicole felt very, very right.

Chapter Five

AROUND SEVEN THAT EVENING, while she was cooking dinner in her apartment, Jay's cell phone rang. "Nicole, could you come here and watch the stove, please?" she called out, running in to the next room to find her phone. It was sitting on the living room coffee table, and the sight of an unfamiliar number instantly made her nervous. Phone calls were hard enough even when she knew who was on the other end. She swiped across the screen and lifted it to her ear as she took a seat on the couch. "Um, hello?"

"Jay...uh, Vinkatissan?"

"Speaking. Who is this?"

"This is Officer Bellows from the police department. Lieutenant Slack told me to call you and tell you..." He paused, and Jay heard the faint sound of shouting and swearing in the background. "Something about a crazy lady trying to gain access to a crime scene? He isn't being really clear right now."

Jay's head lolled onto the back of the couch. She closed her eyes, massaging her forehead with her free hand. *She didn't... No, she did. Of fucking course she did.* "The Fox crime scene, right?"

"Yes."

"Does this lady have funny glasses, bright colored shoes, and a matching purse?"

"As a matter of fact, she does. Do you know what's going on? Because Lieutenant Slack is still yelling. I think his face is turning purple."

"Yeah. Go tell Lieutenant Slack I'm on my way to pick her up." Jay ended the call, setting aside her phone and burying her face in her hands. "Shit," she groaned, fingers pressing hard into her scalp. Her shoulders lifted, and she fought not to shake. "I knew this was going to happen."

"What's wrong?" Jay looked up to see Nicole standing in the

kitchen doorway. Her hair was piled into a messy knot of curls on top of her head, and her brow was creased with worry. Jay deliberately tried to ignore the fact that she was only wearing a pair of purloined boxers and a tank top that rode up past her midriff. She was too wound up to appreciate the view. "I turned the stove down. Do you have to go somewhere?"

"My aunt Mimi went to *investigate* the crime scene. I have to pick her up before they throw her in jail for obstruction of justice or something."

"Do you want me to come with you? Dinner can wait."

Jay chewed on the inside of her cheek and fiddled with her glasses. She knew there was no reason for Nicole to come, but she wanted her nearby anyway. She wasn't sure she could manage this on her own without losing it. "Would you? Please?"

"Of course. Why wouldn't I want to help?"

"Well, my aunt is kind of a pain. And I would understand if you didn't want to see your grandfather's house right now after what happened there last night."

"I think your Aunt Mimi's darling." Nicole padded over to the couch, putting a hand on Jay's shoulder. "And don't worry about taking me back to Grandpa's house. I practically grew up there. I'm sure I can handle it."

"Okay. As long as you aren't sick of me."

Nicole gave her a warm smile and reached out to stroke her cheek. "I could never get sick of you. I'm grateful you're letting me stay here with you. I need to be with someone right now."

"Me too," she whispered, leaning into Nicole's hand.

"Good." Nicole pulled back and ruffled Jay's hair, forcing her to lift her arms in defense and smooth it back down. "Leave it, it looks better that way. Give me a minute to get dressed and turn off the stove, and we'll go get your Aunt Mimi together."

***

Aunt Mimi was already waiting for them at the front gate when Jay drove up. This time, her purse was bright green, and she had shiny lime shoes to match. Her arms were folded tight across her ample chest, the front of her dress was covered with smudges of dirt, and her expression read annoyance.

Lieutenant Slack stood beside her, politely but firmly escorting her to the car. "Good, Bellows called you," he said when Jay rolled down the window. "They found her wandering around in the back yard near the gardening shed. I convinced the officers on the scene not to book her, but you have to take her home. They thought she was from the media. If you haven't noticed, it's a circus out on the main road. None of them can get up to the house. I have no idea how your aunt snuck past us."

"Don't feel bad. Aunt Mimi is..." Jay paused, struggling to find a polite word. "Resourceful. I'll keep her out of your way."

Slack nodded, giving Aunt Mimi a nudge toward the car. "See that you do. We can't have people snooping around out here while we're trying to solve a case. Please, don't come back."

Jay gave Slack an awkward, apologetic wave and rolled up the window, watching carefully to make sure Aunt Mimi actually sat down. It would be just like her aunt to sneak out the other side of the car while Lieutenant Slack wasn't looking.

Fortunately, Mimi didn't make a break for freedom. "Obviously, I should have looked for a more subtle way to access the crime scene," she said once she closed the door. "There are too many police officers around."

"Memma, you can't do this." Jay reversed the car back down the drive to the main road. "It's illegal. You could contaminate evidence."

"Exactly! That's why I need to get in. I have to examine all the evidence left before it gets contaminated."

"Miss Venkatesan—" Nicole started to say.

"Oh, call me Mimi, dear. I told you this morning."

"Well, Mimi, they keep people out of crime scenes for a good reason. What if the murderer or an accomplice tried to remove evidence? They can't let just anyone in."

Jay breathed a sigh of relief. This time it seemed that Nicole was on her side.

Aunt Mimi rolled her eyes. "I know that, dear. But I'm not the murderer or an accomplice. I'm not even involved."

"Exactly," Jay insisted. "You're not involved. So there's no reason for you to come back here."

"But I have to. Who else is going to find out who killed Nicole's grandfather? The police?"

"That's what the police are for." Jay resisted the temptation to bang her head against the steering wheel. Aunt Mimi started in on another rant, but she tuned it out, peering ahead at the edge of the drive. Several news vans were lined up along the side of the road, and she could make out shadowy figures darting between them. A young police officer shined his light in their direction, and she pulled the car to a stop, rolling down the window a second time. "Yes, officer?"

"Oh, it's you. Sorry, it's hard to keep track with all the video crews running around. Go on ahead. I already got your license plate number on the way in."

The delay caught the attention of the crowd. A dozen reporters and cameramen swarmed around the van, trying to get a look at who was inside. "Hey, I know her," someone shouted. "She's one of the grandchildren. Charlie, get some video of this. It's one of the Fox grandkids."

Nicole ducked down in her seat, but it was too late. Several pale faces peered through the passenger's side window, aiming cameras through the glass.

"Oh no," Jay groaned. The swarming reporters had completely blocked their way. She could see the officer on duty talking into his radio, but for the moment, they were stuck. She tried to roll up her window, but in her nervousness, her fingers fumbled over the button.

"I'm sorry, Jay," Nicole said in a quiet, subdued voice. "I should have thought ahead about this."

One woman, pluckier than the rest, forced her way around to the other side of the car. She leaned forward, nearly pushing past Jay's face in an effort to get to Nicole. "Cindy Larson from the *Tribune*. Do you have anything to say about your grandfather's murder, Miss Fox?"

"No comment," Nicole said, raising her voice to be heard over the other questions.

"Are you going to inherit any of your grandfather's mon—"

Jay finally managed to roll up the window and force the woman back, but the muffled questions continued. In desperation, she put the car in park and slammed her foot on the gas, revving the engine. That startled some of the reporters in front of the car, and she shifted back into drive, letting the car crawl forward through the ocean of people. Once they realized the car was moving, the crowd reluctantly parted, letting them nose through to the main road.

"Well," Aunt Mimi huffed once they were clear of the press. "How rude. I'm sorry about that, my dear. That woman was so insensitive about your loss."

Jay turned to stare at her aunt in disbelief, but couldn't find any words to comment on the hypocrisy. Instead, she turned her eyes back to the road and drove away from the Fox Mansion as fast as the speed limit would allow.

"It's all right," Nicole murmured politely. Her voice was unusually soft, and Jay frowned with worry. It wasn't like her normally talkative girlfriend to be at a loss for words, or to speak under her breath.

Aunt Mimi seemed to notice Nicole's somber mood, too, because she offered a smile. "The good news is that I found something. Before the police escorted me out of the gardening shed—" Something in the tone of her aunt's voice convinced Jay that the escorting had been particularly insistent. "I happened to run across some gopher bait tucked away in a corner."

Jay couldn't keep a sour face. Her curiosity got the better of her, and she glanced into the rear view mirror. "So?"

"So, gophers aren't a common pest in the northeastern United States. Even more unusual, the container of food pellets was full, but the bottle of strychnine that went with it had been opened. Recently, too, I think. There wasn't any dust on the box, and the rest of the shed was covered in cobwebs."

"That makes sense," Nicole said. "Grandpa hired a landscaping company to take care of the grounds. None of us have any reason to go back there."

"But someone did. A murderer." Aunt Mimi fidgeted with her purse.

"That's a bit of a stretch—" Jay said.

"It's not a stretch at all. I guessed the murderer might have used strychnine when Nicole described Stephen Fox's symptoms. It isn't common anymore, but it's a classic poison in film and literature, and it causes a uniquely violent reaction. I'm absolutely certain I'm right. When the police finish Mr. Fox's autopsy, I'm sure they'll find a large dose of strychnine in his system."

***

"Now, dear," Aunt Mimi said, tapping her ballpoint pen on a pad of notebook paper, "the first thing to do is line up our suspects. The first symptoms appear ten to twenty minutes after ingesting an overdose of strychnine, so it had to be someone at the party." She ripped a sheet of paper from the pad and slid it across the tabletop to Nicole. "While we list the suspects, would you draw me a picture of the sitting room? A diagram will have to do until I can get a real look."

"A diagram is all you're going to see," Jay protested, but she got out of her seat to find a second pen for Nicole. "If you want me to make her leave, just tell me," she said as she passed, leaning down to whisper in Nicole's ear.

"It's all right," Nicole whispered back while Aunt Mimi scribbled and mumbled to herself. "She isn't hurting anyone. And who knows? Maybe she'll find something no one has caught. She did find the gopher bait in the garden shed, after all."

"A theory that's yet to be proven." Despite the mounting evidence, Jay was still reluctant to follow along with Aunt Mimi and Nicole's theories. Her morbid mind only needed the slightest push to stumble on an awful idea and run with it, and it was taking everything she had to cling to logic while they speculated. "Besides, wouldn't gopher poison taste awful? He probably would have noticed that if someone slipped it in his drink."

Aunt Mimi looked up from her work. "That's a good point. Strychnine is a very bitter poison, hard to disguise."

"Not for Grandpa, unfortunately," Nicole said. "He was in treatment for cancer awhile back, and the radiation dulled his sense of taste. That's why the Fox Foundation's funding for cancer research got increased." A sad smile crossed her face, and her lips quivered. "He was probably just drinking the alcohol for a bit of a buzz, the old lush. He'd been in remission for almost five years…"

"He sounds like he was a very special man," Aunt Mimi said to Nicole, surprising Jay with the display of sympathy. "Why don't you draw the room for me, dear? Maybe it will help."

Jay peered over Nicole's shoulder, watching as she began to sketch out the scene of the crime. She started with a square, using the lines of the notebook paper as a guide, and filled it in with boxes for furniture and stick figures for people. Finally, she drew a big 'x' where her grandfather had collapsed.

"This isn't going to work," Nicole sighed, setting the pen down. "I can't remember where everyone was standing. No one stayed in one part of the room for long. They all moved around and talked with each other."

"Then we'll just have to assume anyone could have slipped the strychnine into your grandfather's drink while he wasn't looking." Aunt Mimi studied Nicole's diagram, peering over the tops of her horn-rimmed glasses. "This is actually very helpful. It should do perfectly for now."

Curiously, Jay looked at Aunt Mimi's own paper. The top was titled

'List of Suspects', and beneath it was a single row of names.

Thomas Fox Sr.—Stephen Fox's son (unlikely suspect, out of town during party)
Beatrice, his wife
Thomas Junior, his first son
Patrick, his second son

Martha Rorsche—Stephen Fox's daughter
William, her husband
Denise, her daughter

Gregory Fox—Stephen Fox's son
Janine, his wife
Nicole, his daughter
Harry, his son

Jay Venkatesan, Nicole's guest
Household staff (unlikely, not in the same room)

"Hey, why's my name on there? And Nicole's?"

"Because you're suspects, of course," Aunt Mimi sighed, as if it was the most obvious thing in the world. "I can't leave anyone out, can I?" Jay started to protest, but she didn't get the chance. Aunt Mimi barreled on. "I suppose the most obvious motive is money. Everyone at the party except for you stood to inherit."

Nicole frowned. "Any member of the family could have asked Grandpa for a loan. He would have given it to them. And most of them have plenty of money of their own."

"You never know what secret debts wealthy people have. For all we know, one of your uncles, aunts, or cousins might have a secret vice."

Jay rubbed the back of her neck. "That's a little dramatic, Aunt Mimi—"

"There's only one other motive I can think of, and that's a family grudge." She turned back to Nicole. "Tell me, dear, did all your other relatives get along?"

Nicole's pleasant smile twitched. For once, she wasn't quick with an answer. She remained silent for several moments, considering her words carefully. "Our family has its fair share of skeletons, but nothing involving Grandpa. As far as I know, he didn't have any secrets. Everyone loved him."

"All right. For now, we'll assume money was the primary motive. The next step will be to interview the suspects."

Jay instantly tensed up. "Memma, no." Her voice was lost in the conversation.

"I can help with that." Nicole's excitement returned as she leaned over the table. "I'm sure I could get Harry to meet with you, and Aunt Martha never shuts up. Aunt Beatrice will cooperate if I get her drunk enough."

"Wonderful!" Aunt Mimi clapped her hands together. "What about the other guests?"

"My cousins won't be much help. Denise is an idiot, Patrick's always busy, and Tom Junior's an ass. But maybe there's a way you could meet my parents."

"Exactly what I was thinking. You should invite Nicole's parents over for dinner, Jay. Since you were invited to Nicole's grandfather's birthday—"

"He was murdered. I don't think it counts."

"It's only polite to return the invitation. I'm sure Nicole's parents want to learn all about you anyway."

Jay swallowed. The last thing she wanted to do was have dinner with Nicole's parents in the middle of a murder investigation. Adding Aunt Mimi into the mix only made things worse. She looked at Nicole, hoping for a little support, but her girlfriend didn't seem to notice her terrified expression.

"Okay," Nicole said, and Jay's stomach sank. "I'll invite my parents over here for dinner in a few days. You can drop by, and we'll invite you in. But please, try to be subtle. If Mum Janine realizes something's up, you won't get anything out of her."

Aunt Mimi laughed. "If Holmes and Poirot can be subtle, so can I."

"This is a terrible idea," Jay mumbled, but she had long since given up. Aunt Mimi and Nicole were stubborn on their own, but together, they were impossible to argue with. While they continued planning, she pulled out her phone and started working on a grocery list. She would have to buy food and cleaning supplies if she was going to host Nicole's parents. She doubted she would make it through the night without humiliating herself, but at least she could make sure her place didn't look like a pigsty.

Chapter Six

"ARE YOU SURE SHE wasn't bothering you?" Jay circled around the back of the couch, resting her hands on Nicole's shoulders from behind. She gave the tense muscles a testing squeeze, trying to work out some of the stiffness. "Aunt Mimi's a lot to handle on a normal day. I wouldn't blame you if you asked me to send her away next time."

Nicole groaned and slumped forward, closing her eyes. "Keep doing that and I won't let you stop. No, your Aunt Mimi didn't bother me at all. With the police keeping quiet, it's actually a relief to talk to someone about it."

Jay hooked her thumbs under Nicole's shoulder blades, rubbing in firm circles. "Even if that someone is a murder mystery fanatic who's never solved a real crime in her life?"

"Yes, even then. Besides, my family is way crazier than yours at the moment." Nicole sighed and reached back, squeezing one of her hands. "It's been a relief to stay here with you, Jay. I've needed support these past few days. We've only been dating two months. A lot of people would have cut and run."

Jay tugged the tie out of Nicole's hair, letting her curls fall free down the back of her neck. She dipped down and placed a kiss on top of Nicole's head, inhaling the flowery scent of her shampoo. "I'm not most people," she whispered against the silky strands. "And I like having you here. It's not an inconvenience." Despite the tragic circumstances, it was nice to have Nicole around in the mornings and evenings. She hadn't known sharing an apartment could feel so comfortable. Being around other people usually sapped her energy, but Nicole's presence nourished her instead. She had never felt so relaxed around a romantic partner before.

Nicole turned around, still holding her hand. "Well, I'm glad you don't think I'm an inconvenience, but I was hoping for something a little sweeter."

"Well, I know we're good at sleeping together," Jay said. Nicole stared at her, and she hurried to correct herself. "I mean, we sleep on different sides of the bed, and you're the right size to spoon, and...I'll shut up now."

"I'm just glad you don't snore." Nicole turned back around, shrugging her shoulders once. Jay got the message and continued rubbing on either side of her spine. "Ow! Yes, that's where it hurts...riiight there..." She practically purred as a knot beside her shoulder blade loosened, hanging her head so her hair fell around her face. "And for the record, I'm pretty sure we'll be compatible in bed. And in the shower. And on the kitchen table. And wherever else we feel like having sex once you put the moves on me."

Jay swallowed nervously. Since coming to stay at her apartment, Nicole had lived in tank tops and stolen boxers, or oversized shirts with no bottoms at all. Taking it slow was becoming difficult, but at the same time, she was anxious about initiating a more intimate relationship. Even with someone as considerate as Nicole, sex was guaranteed to be messy and awkward and mildly terrifying. She wasn't sure she could handle the added stress on top of everything else.

Reluctantly, she stroked the side of Nicole's arm before pulling away. "There. You're done."

Nicole pulled her feet up onto the couch, turning around to look at her again. "What's wrong? I didn't come on too strong, did I?"

"No." Nicole gave her a doubtful look, and Jay bit her lower lip. She had to say something. "Okay, part of me is dying to have sex with you. You're beautiful and nice and you smell *really* good and I can't stop staring at you, especially when you're wearing my clothes. But I'd feel like a total creep if I initiated sex right now. Your grandpa just died. You've been crying a lot these past few days. It doesn't feel like the right time. And to be honest, I'm really worried I'll do something to screw it up. I've only had a couple of girlfriends before you, and that was more years ago than I want to admit. I'll probably forget what to do and freak out or something..."

To her surprise, Nicole turned around and shifted onto her knees, leaning over the back of the couch. A finger pressed over her mouth, stopping the stream of worries that spilled from Jay's lips. "You're sweet, Jay, but you worry too much. I loved my grandpa with all my heart, but he had nothing to do with my sex life when he was alive, and I want to keep it that way now. So..." She leaned forward, and Jay's heart flew up into her throat. "When you're ready to find out just how sexually compatible we are, let me know. I won't think any less of you for being nervous."

"Yeah..." The word cracked, and Jay coughed before trying again. "I mean, sure. I'll...I'll do that."

"Good." Nicole folded a hand around the back of Jay's neck, and before she knew what was happening, warm lips covered hers. She stiffened, then groaned into the kiss, closing her eyes as Nicole's fingers threaded through her hair. Her hands shot down to Nicole's shoulders, clinging for dear life until they finally broke apart.

"Wow."

"Yeah. Wow."

They stared at each other for several breathless seconds. Jay pulled back, and her face split in a wide grin. "Okay. So. Dinner? Any thoughts?" Before Nicole could answer, Jay's pocket started buzzing. Her brow wrinkled, and she pulled out her phone, sighing when she recognized the number. "Or maybe not. Lieutenant Slack is calling. Let me see what he wants."

***

"Miss Vincatessan, welcome back," Slack said as he took the empty chair on the other side of the table. Jay gave him a slightly forced smile. She was getting tired of this routine, but at least the lieutenant was polite about it. "Your aunt didn't drive you here, did she? Please tell me I'm not going to find her snooping around the building."

Jay sighed, hanging her head in embarrassment. She could easily picture her Aunt Mimi peeking through windows and badgering the poor receptionist at the front desk. "Not today, sir. Hopefully, she'll stay out of your hair from now on."

"I don't suppose she told you what she was doing in the garden shed, did she? It's not even connected to the house."

After a moment's hesitation, Jay decided that she might as well come clean with the Lieutenant on the off chance that Aunt Mimi's hunch was right. "She was looking for poison, and she thinks she found some. Apparently, she noticed an open bottle of strychnine next to a full container of gopher bait."

She half-expected Lieutenant Slack to laugh, but instead, his eyes widened with shock. He sat up straighter and leaned across the table. "Wait, strychnine?"

Jay bit her lip. "I'm guessing you got the autopsy report back." *She was right, wasn't she? Damn it, I hate it when she's right. The crazy, awful thoughts in my head are supposed to stay there, not turn out to be real.*

"Exactly. We see it a lot, but not for homicides. It's an ingredient in old pesticides. You know, things with warning labels that have been in your mom's garage for ten or fifteen years. It's definitely not what most people would think to spike a drink with if they wanted to kill someone."

"Why not?"

"Well, it's bitter for one..."

"That's what Aunt Mimi said, too. Apparently, Stephen Fox had cancer a few years ago. The radiation treatment dulled his sense of taste."

"And that points to the family again. Most of them probably knew." There was a pause, and Lieutenant Slack's face grew thoughtful. "Here's what bothers me about all this. Strychnine isn't a nice poison. About twenty minutes after it's taken, the victim gets uncontrollable convulsions. Next, terrible pain. Finally, your respiratory system shuts off. You can't breathe no matter how hard you try. It's a gruesome way to die."

Jay sat up straighter in her chair. Her stomach lurched as she remembered the way Mr. Fox had fallen to the floor. *The way his eyes fogged over...the way he clutched his chest...*Once again, her mind flashed to Nicole's face, contorted in agony. Her hands started to tremble in her lap. "Why are you telling me this?"

Slack paced back around to his side of the table, resting his arms on the other empty chair. "Because you're the closest thing I've got to an unbiased witness. Someone wanted to *hurt* Stephen Fox, not just kill him. Any thoughts about who that person might be?"

"I...I'm not sure." Jay's teeth wanted to chatter even though it wasn't cold, so she clenched them together. "I don't know the family secrets. You should ask Nicole."

"That's my next stop. But your girlfriend's part of the Fox family, too. She has her own secrets and biases, just like the rest of them. She might not see things as clearly as you."

"But I didn't see anything," Jay protested. The pain in her chest was back, sharp stabs right through her breastbone. "If it was poison in his glass, I'm sure Nicole didn't do it. I was with her the whole time."

"The whole time?" Slack's hands curled tighter around the chair. "Are you sure?"

"Well, I got lost in the halls and ran into Tom Junior, but that was before we went to the sitting room."

Slack's large shoulders bristled, and Jay was reminded of a dog that had just caught a scent. "Tom Junior. Was anyone else with him when you ran into each other in the hallway?" She shook her head. "Was he carrying anything?" She shook her head a second time. "Did he tell you what he was doing there?"

"No. I didn't ask."

"Right." Slack scooped up the file from the table and tucked it under his arm, gathering his coat in the other. "I'll be back in a few minutes, Miss Vincatessin. Please wait here."

Jay waited in silence until the Lieutenant left. She tried not to think about what he had said, but her mind was stuck in a terrifying loop. *Except for my trip to the bathroom, we spent the entire night within arm's reach. We were together in the sitting room for longer than twenty minutes, weren't we? There's no way she could have...Shit. I'm a horrible person for even considering it.*

But something had been off about Nicole's face when Aunt Mimi mentioned family secrets. Jay could remember the awkward angle of her smile. *No. This is my anxiety talking. Just because I'm having a bad thought doesn't mean it's true. The probability that Nicole killed her grandfather is vanishingly small... even though I wasn't with her the entire night... and even though she knew he didn't have a sense of taste...*

"Oh God," Jay groaned, resting her face on the table and closing her eyes. The worst possible scenario was stuck in her head once again, and she couldn't dislodge it. Instead of watching Nicole writhe in pain, she imagined a pale hand slipping something into Mr. Fox's drink. *No. I know Nicole. She's not a killer. She loved her grandpa. I need to stop thinking like Aunt Mimi and let the police do their job.* But no matter how hard she tried, she couldn't get the questions to go away.

***

"Well, that was the most pointless interview ever," Nicole huffed. She rummaged through her purse for her keys, and a swift jerk of her elbow nearly landed in the middle of Jay's stomach. She dodged away just in time, taking a cautious step backward. She wanted to offer comfort, but not from the danger zone.

"What did Lieutenant Slack say to you? You were pretty quiet on the car ride." Quiet wasn't exactly the right word. Nicole had made plenty of noises on the drive, but most of them were sighs and grunts. It was unlike her to be so non-verbal.

"I'm not sure I want to talk about it." Nicole found her keys and shoved them into the lock. "I just want to go in my house, grab my mail and some fresh clothes, and get out of here. You don't mind if I stay another night, right?" She turned, and some of the stiffness seeped from her posture. "I...I'm not ready to be alone yet."

Jay wrapped an arm around Nicole's shoulders. She was still a little nervous in Nicole's presence after her minor freak-out in the interview room, but she recognized that it was her problem. Nicole hadn't done anything wrong, and she needed to keep being supportive until her crazy spell wore off. Fortunately, faking like everything was normal was a skill she had been forced to develop. "Of course I don't mind. You can stay as long as you want."

Nicole hung her head. "Thanks. I'm sorry I'm so grumpy. Slack just kept asking about grudges and family secrets. That's literally the phrase he used. 'Family secrets.' Yeah, sure, every family has its secrets, but no one wanted to hurt Grandpa. I told Slack all of us loved him, but he just kept looking at me like he didn't believe me."

"Well?" Jay asked as they stepped inside. "Should he believe you?"

Nicole tensed beneath her arm. "Of course. I told him everything I knew, everything I could remember. I've been to three interviews so far, and his questions are always the same. I don't know what he expects to get out of me anymore."

Jay remained quiet and gazed around the front room, staring up at the ceiling. Nicole's house wasn't as extravagant as the Fox mansion, but it was fairly large. Most people their age were still apartment-bound. She had been a little intimidated the first time Nicole had invited her inside.

"Come on," Nicole sighed, "let's go in. I want to drop this mail off and pack a fresh bag." She held up a bulging stack of envelopes and snapped it through the air. "Actually, why don't you take it in and grab a snack? I need a minute in the bathroom."

Jay understood that request immediately. Nicole wanted to be alone. It stung a little, but she understood. She had never seen Nicole use such an introverted strategy for coping, but she had never seen Nicole this angry before, either. "Sure," she said, taking the envelopes and giving Nicole a quick kiss on the forehead. "I'll wait for you in the kitchen. Take as long as you need."

Several minutes later, she sat alone at Nicole's kitchen table, fidgeting awkwardly in her chair. Desperate to do something with her hands, and bored of the games on her phone, she began sorting through the large pile of mail. She threw bills in one pile, credit card offers in a second pile, and everything else in a third pile. "Why do you have so much mail, Nicky?"

"What?" a voice drifted in from the hall. Jay grinned a little. Apparently, Nicole had supersonic bat hearing. She walked in from the next room in a fluffy robe and wearing a towel piled on top of her head like a turban. "Sorry I took so long. I decided to grab a shower. Oh, thanks for helping with that. I didn't really feel like going through it."

"Yeah," Jay said, a little shyly. She hadn't expected Nicole to catch her in the act. Even though she hadn't opened any of the letters, she didn't want to come off as nosy. One snoop in the family was bad enough. "You don't mind, right?"

"Of course not." Nicole picked up the pile of business letters and flicked through them with slightly damp fingers, leaving a few wet prints on the envelopes. "Electric bill, cable bill, water bill...argh, I hate bills!" She tossed them back onto the table without opening them. "The worst part is, I always pay them on time and request online statements. I don't know why they still send the paper ones, too...Wait, this one's weird." She held up a large brown envelope, and Jay saw that it was addressed from the county. She stood up to look over Nicole's shoulder and see what it was, but Nicole said it out loud first. "Oh wow. It's Grandpa's will."

Jay stared at her in confusion. "They send wills in the mail?"

"Yup. Will readings are only for TV, you goober. In real life, they just send it to you in the mail. Actually, anyone can look up a will in their county, even if they're not related to the will's author. That's why I was so annoyed with Harry the other day for acting like it was a big secret..." Her voice drifted off as she continued reading, and her face tightened. "This is about what I expected. Liquid monetary assets go to my father, Aunt Martha, and Uncle Tom. Most of the company shares are going to my father. He always had the most business sense. The interest from the trust—oh that's more than I expected—is going to me, Harry, Denise, Patrick, and Tom Junior. They'll just blow it all, but if I save mine, I'll be set for a long time."

"So, you don't have to work anymore?"

Nicole looked away from the paper and met her eyes. "Have to? That depends. I have to work, but not for money. I'd go crazy if I stayed home all the time, and however much I complain, I like working at the Fox Foundation." She looked back down at the packet and turned to the third page. "Denise and I get some of Grandma's old jewelry, there are some big donations to charity, and—oh!" She sat back down in her chair, completely stunned. "Oh my God."

Gently, Jay took the packet from Nicole's limp hand, reading it for herself. "Your grandpa willed you the entire Fox Foundation?"

"Yeah," Nicole mumbled. "He did. I mean, it's a non-profit, so I don't get much of a salary, but that's a lot of power. I get to make major decisions about how to allocate the funds. The Fox Foundation was Grandpa's baby. I can't believe he's trusting me with it."

Jay stared at Nicole in shock. Horrible thoughts swirled through her head. *What if Nicole...?* No, she couldn't think like that. *But what if?* She took a deep breath. *I'm Nicole's girlfriend. Things are getting serious, and trust is a big part of that. What does it say about our relationship, and me as a person, if I can't trust her? I need to get over this, fast.* Gently, she set the packet back down on the table. She had to ignore it. That was the only way. Maybe if she ignored her doubts long enough, they would disappear.

"Jay, are you all right?" Nicole asked. A worried hand reached out, resting on top of hers.

Jay jerked away, startled by the touch. The hurt look on Nicole's face tore at her heart. "I'm sorry," she said in a low voice. "You startled me. I didn't expect to be dating an heiress."

Nicole pressed her lips together. "I was an heiress before tonight."

"It's just a lot, you know? For you too, I bet."

Nicole looked unconvinced, but did not push further. A knot formed in Jay's throat. She hated herself for thinking such terrible things. "Why don't you call your parents? Find a time for them to come to dinner at my place, and I'll clear my schedule. I..." To her surprise, she realized that part of her had wanted to say *I love you*. But she couldn't give herself over to those feelings until she was sure, absolutely positive, that Nicole hadn't had anything to do with the murder of Mr. Fox.

Chapter Seven

JAY STARED DOWN AT her book, frowning in concentration. She had been stuck on the same page for at least ten minutes, but the words still didn't make any sense. Her thoughts swirled between Nicole and Aunt Mimi, and her stomach was in knots over their ridiculous plan. Even though they had promised not to embarrass her, she doubted either of them knew what they were doing. She sighed and gave up, slamming the book shut. "This is bad," she mumbled, curling into a ball on top of the couch.

"Hopefully you don't mean my lasagna," Nicole said from the direction of the kitchen.

Jay forced herself to look up. For once, Nicole was wearing more than the bare minimum of clothes. Jeans and a sweater weren't exactly a dinner party outfit, but at least she hadn't stolen another pair of boxers. "Thanks for cooking," she said, trying not to stare for too long. "I appreciate it."

Nicole folded her arms, shifting her hip to one side. "I owed you one. You've been letting me stay here since Grandpa died. I'm surprised I haven't worn out my welcome over the past week and a half."

The sound of the doorbell interrupted the conversation. "I'll get it." Jay rolled off the couch and dragged herself toward the door. She paused, running a nervous hand through her hair and straightening her collar. She had chosen to wear something slightly more feminine in the hopes of impressing Nicole's parents. Her tight khaki pants showed off her hips for a change, and her blue blouse had a woman's cut. Satisfied that she looked halfway presentable, she peered through the peephole.

The first thing she saw on the other side of the door was Harry's large grin. Just beyond his shoulders, she could make out Janine and Gregory Fox. Both of them were dressed a little fancier than she had expected, and a nervous pool of sweat started to gather at the base of her spine. She realized that she was gawking and hurried to undo the lock, welcoming Nicole's family inside.

"Hallo, Vinnie!" Harry pulled her into a one-armed hug. "Thanks for having us over. When's dinner? I'm starved."

"Harry..." Janine shot him a disapproving look. Jay noticed that she was dressed in black, and her make-up was understated. It was a departure from the eye-catching dresses she and everyone else had worn at Mr. Fox's birthday party, more appropriate for someone in mourning.

"What? Vinnie likes me. Don't you, Vinnie? And look, I even picked the right clothes." He gestured down at his jeans. "I told you it wasn't formal. I'm as depressed as everyone else about Grandpa, but he wouldn't want us all walking around like we were still at his funeral."

Jay sucked her lower lip between her teeth. "It's all fine. There's no dress code or anything."

"Hello, Miss Ven...uh, Jay," said Gregory. Jay sighed as Nicole's father talked his way around her last name, but she wasn't surprised. "Honestly, I'm not sure what to call you. Nicole's been no help."

"Jay's fine." She gave him a hesitant smile. Gregory didn't seem very excited to see her, but that was to be expected under the circumstances. Mostly, he seemed sad. Like Nicole, it was apparent from his face that he hadn't been getting much sleep.

Reluctantly, Jay turned toward the only remaining member of the party. "And hello, Mrs. Fox. I'm glad you came."

"I'm glad you invited us," Janine said. "Nicole knows she has an open invitation to come stay with us, but she said she was more comfortable here. I...appreciate the effort you've made to support her since last week."

The words of approval came as a surprise. They were a strange departure from Janine's former coldness, and Jay wasn't entirely sure how to respond. *Wow, I'm a really lousy person, tricking a mourning family into coming over just so Aunt Mimi can 'investigate'. This might actually top imagining Nicole as a murderer. At least I've managed to keep that in my head so far.*

Eventually, Jay realized that Janine was waiting for some kind of response. "Um, thank you? We should probably go to the kitchen. Nicole, could you..." She turned around, and her stomach sank. Nicole had disappeared. "I guess she's setting the table. This way." She led the Foxes to the kitchen in awkward silence. Nicole turned away from the stove when they entered, and Jay was so relieved to see her that she stepped in for a hug without thinking. "*Please* don't leave me alone

50

again," she whispered in Nicole's ear. "You know I'm terrible at this."

"Sorry," Nicole whispered back, skimming the side of her cheek. "I was just texting Aunt Mimi. She's about five minutes away."

Jay sighed and the painful knot in her chest pulled even tighter. The past week had just been stress on top of stress. "I never should have agreed to this."

Nicole gave her arm a reassuring squeeze as she went to greet her parents. "Dad, Mom, it's good to see you. And Harry," she added, giving her brother a toothy grin. She reached up to ruffle his hair. "You look like you showered."

Harry slapped her hand away. "Hey. I take excellent care of my hair. How do you think I get dates?"

"Hopefully by keeping your mouth shut. I'm surprised they don't run away as soon as you start talking."

"Right now, my mouth wants some of that lasagna. Give it here." He grabbed a plate from the kitchen counter and wandered over to the stove, serving himself a generous slice.

"Go ahead," Nicole said, smiling at her parents. "This isn't formal. And you really didn't have to dress up..."

Sensing an opportunity to be useful, and more importantly, to escape the conversation, Jay hurried over to the stove and took the four remaining plates. "No, I'll take care of it. Why don't you sit down? Can I get you something to drink?" Both of Nicole's parents hesitated, and her stomach lurched when she realized why. Of course they were wary about letting her make the drinks. Lieutenant Slack didn't think she was much of a suspect, but to the Foxes, she was the only person at the party who wasn't family. They probably thought she had poisoned Mr. Fox so Nicole could receive her inheritance.

"I'll get it," Nicole said stiffly, brushing their fingers together as she passed. Jay breathed in deep through her nose. At least her girlfriend trusted her, which was more than she could say for herself. The nagging thought that Nicole had murdered her grandfather still popped into her head every once in a while, no matter how hard she tried to suppress it.

She busied herself with the plates while Nicole's parents joined Harry at the table. "So, Jay," Gregory said. "Is that your full name?"

Jay's cheeks heated up. The night had just gone from bad to worse. "No," she said, carrying the plates over to the table. "But it's what everyone calls me."

A delighted look crossed Harry's face. He leaned forward over the table, grinning up at her. "Don't tell me you have two unpronounceable names. What is it?"

"Well..."

Nicole gave her an amused look, and she blushed even deeper, certain that she was turning purple. "Really? Jay isn't your full name? I had no idea."

"Um, I..." She almost jumped out of her skin when the doorbell rang again. She glanced at the microwave clock. Aunt Mimi was early, and for once, Jay was actually grateful for the interruption. "I'll see who it is." She quickly made her escape, retracing her steps to the front door.

A quick check through the peephole confirmed that it was indeed Aunt Mimi outside. Even though the image was blurry, the matching powder blue shoes and purse were a dead giveaway. She opened the door. "Aunt Mimi, what a surprise," she said, loud enough so that her voice would carry back into the kitchen. "I wasn't expecting you. Why are you here?"

"You're a terrible actress," Aunt Mimi said with a disapproving frown. "Hopefully Nicole has more talent. You picked a good one, dear."

A little of Jay's embarrassment vanished. "Yeah, I did, didn't I?"

"Stop mooning and introduce me."

Jay obeyed, leading her back to the kitchen and slinking off to the side.

"Hello! You must be Nicole's family," Aunt Mimi said, studying all three dinner guests over the tops of her thick, horn-rimmed glasses. "I'm sorry. You don't have any idea who I am, do you? I'm Jay's Aunt Mimi. My car was having trouble, and when I realized my favorite niece was a few blocks away..."

"I'm your only niece," Jay sighed.

Aunt Mimi glared at her. "As I was saying, I just thought I'd wait here while I called for a tow."

"That sucks," Nicole said, looking appropriately upset. "You're okay though, right? You should stay and have some dinner."

Jay began to have doubts. As relieved as she was to be out of the spotlight, she didn't want Aunt Mimi to make herself comfortable. A few minutes to scope out the suspects was one thing, but a whole dinner? The thought made her feel sick. "Actually, I think—"

"It's the polite thing to do." Nicole gave her a look. "Please, stay. I made enough lasagna for everyone."

Aunt Mimi gave Nicole a brilliant smile. "Thank you, dear. As long as I'm not butting in."

"By all means," Harry said in a cheerful voice. "The more the merrier. You're the first member of Jay's family we've met."

"Hopefully not the last," Aunt Mimi said, taking a seat at the table. "You must be Nicole's brother, Harry. I've been spending a lot of time with your sister lately. She's always over at Jay's apartment." Jay winced at the uncomfortable looks Nicole's parents gave her, but Aunt Mimi didn't seem to notice. Instead, she plowed forward. "It was a little strange at first, especially with all the things I've been reading in the news."

Jay covered her face with her hand. She couldn't imagine a less subtle way to bring up the topic of Mr. Fox's death. "Can we please not talk about this?" she begged, but Aunt Mimi completely ignored her.

"It's been crazy," Harry said, filling the awkward silence. "Reporters are parked outside Grandpa's house all the time. Some of them even stopped by my place the other day, trying to get an interview."

"Damn reporters," Gregory said. "Can't get a moment's peace. They don't even have the decency to wait until after the burial."

"I agree with Jay," Janine said quietly. "Perhaps now isn't the best time to talk about Stephen."

"Nicole always spoke very fondly of him," Aunt Mimi interrupted. "She was so shaken up when she told me about the night he died."

"I'll go get some more lasagna," Jay muttered, eager to excuse herself. She could sense that things were about to escalate, and she didn't want any part in it.

Harry waved at her. "More for me too, please, if you don't mind. Anyway, the police haven't let us claim his body. They also haven't told us anything yet. Guess it's not surprising, since they think one of us killed him."

Janine gasped in surprise. She narrowed her eyes at Harry. "Don't talk like that, especially in front of..."

"Come on, Mom. He was crying out in pain. It wasn't some stupid seizure like you keep telling everyone."

Jay sighed, trying to block out their argument. This was going even worse than expected.

"The police were pretty clear when they talked to me," Nicole said. "I'm sure he didn't just have a seizure."

Gregory pushed his plate aside. Janine set down her glass, staring at a blank space on the wall. Jay read their pained looks and decided to intercede one last time. "Aunt Mimi, I know you're curious, but maybe you should ask questions about this later? Someone died. His family is still recovering from that loss."

"Exactly," said Aunt Mimi. "Someone died. All the more reason to ask questions."

"So, you think it's a murder, too?" Harry asked.

"I wasn't there," Aunt Mimi pointed out. "I can only formulate a hypothesis at this point."

"Of course it wasn't a murder," Janine insisted. "That would suggest someone in the family..." Her voice trailed off as she realized that everyone else around the table was looking at her. "All of you really think that someone in the family murdered him? You can't possibly believe it."

"I'm sure the police will sort it out," Jay pleaded, but no one seemed to hear her. Since none of her guests were eating anymore, she started gathering up the plates. "I'll bring out dessert and refill those drinks." There was another painful silence. "Or maybe just the dessert."

"So, you say you know Jay's aunt, Nicole?" Janine asked as Jay stood up to get the cheesecake.

"Yes, I know Aunt Mimi..."

Don't connect me to her, please, Jay thought desperately, wishing with all her might. If she was lucky, Nicole's parents would classify Mimi as a distant, eccentric relative, one with only a minor presence in her life. Her hands shook as she took the cheesecake out of the refrigerator, and she almost dropped it onto the floor.

"She and Jay are very close."

Damn.

Janine frowned. "Then why is she really here, asking questions about our family?"

"Because her car broke down," Nicole said calmly.

"I consider that highly unlikely."

"I don't blame her for being curious," said Harry. "With all the news coverage, what do you expect? Of course she wants to ask questions. We all should be asking a lot more questions about this whole thing. Something's wrong with it."

"Those damn reporters, that's what's wrong. I can't even get my car out of the driveway to get to work. Ugh, work! Running the business is a headache. I almost wish he hadn't left it to me, but Tom and Martha can't find their way out of a paper bag, let alone run a company." Everyone turned to look at Gregory. He stiffened, realizing that he was being scrutinized. "Well...it's true."

Jay set his cheesecake down in front of him and hurried back to her seat.

"What I want to know about is the yellow garter," Aunt Mimi said, completely ignoring her dessert. "Why was it lying next to the body?"

"How do you know about that?" Janine snapped. "What's your involvement in this?"

Nicole stood up, resting her hands on the table. "Mom, don't..."

"She's not involved," Jay said, desperate to salvage what she could from the conversation. She had honestly wanted to impress Nicole's family, and had hoped that, for once, Aunt Mimi would be discreet. She should have known better. "She's just delusional. For some reason, she thinks she can 'solve the mystery.'"

Aunt Mimi, who had a rhinoceros hide to go with her ego, didn't seem offended at all by her comments. "Are you done yet, Jay? Really. Calling your aunt delusional! I should tell your mother."

Jay groaned. "Please, don't."

"There are more of you?" Harry asked, looking pleased. "Great. Your aunt's really entertaining, Vinnie."

"I'm glad someone's enjoying themselves," Jay said under her breath.

Janine snatched her purse from beneath the table and stood up. Her eyes flashed, and she held her shoulders in a stiff, straight line. "Thank you for dinner, Nicole, but I think your father and I should get home. You can come and see us later. Alone."

Nicole's forehead tightened with disappointment, but she nodded her head. "Right. Sure. Do you want me to send some of that cheesecake with you? Because I could..." One look at her stepmother's face made her backtrack. "Okay. I'll call you tomorrow?"

"Maybe the day after," Gregory said as Janine headed for the front door. "And if you don't mind, I'd like some of that cheesecake."

"Here," Nicole said, passing him the rest of the dish. "Take the whole thing. My appetite's gone."

"I think I'll stay for a bit," Harry volunteered around a mouthful of cake. He remained in his seat, still working on his slice. "Nicky won't mind. Right?"

Nicole sighed. "I guess. Bye, Dad." She leaned in for an awkward hug, then watched her father hurry after Janine. Once he was gone, she slumped back into her seat, lowering her forehead onto the table. "This was a terrible idea."

Chapter Eight

"TERRIBLE?" AUNT MIMI SAID incredulously. "Not at all. I found out much more than I expected from that conversation."

Jay stared down at her shoes. She knew better than to ask.

"I think terrible is about the right word." Harry pushed his empty plate aside, and Jay scooped it up automatically, carrying it to the kitchen sink. "I mean, it could have gone worse, but still. Terrible sums it up."

Nicole remained slumped over the table. "I just don't see the point. We didn't learn anything new. I don't know why I thought my parents would know anything useful anyway." She turned, and the disappointment in her eyes made Jay pause. "I'm really sorry, Jay. I should have listened to you."

Although it was tempting to deliver an I-told-you-so, she gave Nicole a forgiving smile instead. She left the rest of the dirty dishes in the sink and returned to the table, resting her hands on top of Nicole's shoulders. She gave them a gentle squeeze, and Nicole finally lifted her head.

"So, why did you arrange all this?" Harry asked. "We all know someone killed Grandpa, but I didn't expect you to go for the throat like that. You don't think Dad or Mum Janine killed him, do you?"

Aunt Mimi shook her head, even though the question had not been directed at her. "No. At least, I don't think your father has anything to do with this. He seems almost irritated that Stephen Fox died and left him with the family business."

"That sounds like Dad," Nicole admitted. "Deflect, deflect, deflect. He's exactly the type of person that would focus on problems at work to avoid thinking about what happened. I know it's hard to tell, but losing Grandpa hit him pretty hard."

Harry voiced what all of them were thinking. "If not Dad, then who?"

Jay surprised herself by offering her own theory. With Nicole's parents gone, she didn't feel quite so inhibited. "I can't believe I'm saying this, but I'm suspicious of Tom Junior. I saw him sneaking around in the hallway before we all went to the sitting room. He could have been getting something..."

"Like the strychnine from the garden shed," Nicole said.

"Maybe. But I could be biased. He wasn't exactly nice to me when we first met."

"Tom's smart enough to think of something like that," Harry said, nodding in agreement. "He's one of the only people in our family bright enough to think of poison, to be honest. Unfortunately, some of our other relatives are lacking in the brain department."

Aunt Mimi's eyes glinted with interest behind her horn-rimmed glasses. "Really? Who are you referring to, Harry?"

"Well, Aunt Martha's a flighty hypochondriac. I'd count her out, despite her weird obsession with her own impending death. She's not smart enough to come up with a murder plot like this. Uncle Tom's no fool, but he was out of the country."

"Uncle Tom's back now," Nicole said coldly. "Dad texted me earlier. Apparently, he was very upset that this mess pulled him away from his wonderful time in Paris."

"Right," Harry said. "Moving on. Denise isn't smart enough to think of poison, and Aunt Beatrice is a raging drunk. I'd be surprised if she could have poured her own drinks by the end of the night, let alone poison Grandpa's. That leaves Mum Janine, Uncle Bill, Patrick and Tom Junior, and us. Oh, and Jay I suppose, but I don't see what good killing Grandpa would have done her."

Jay gave him a small smile of thanks, still running her hand over the curve of Nicole's shoulder.

"You're including yourself on the list of suspects?" Aunt Mimi asked, looking at Harry with surprise and a little admiration.

Harry shrugged. "Well, I was there. So was Nicky. Either of us could have gotten close enough to do it. Anyone could have, really. I think we should start by looking at the people bright enough to think of poison."

"We?" Jay repeated warily. *Oh no, not another addition to the Amateur Sleuthing Club. Things are already bad enough.*

"Yes, we. I loved Grandpa. You don't think I'm going to let you three look into everyone else without me, do you?"

Nicole's sad look finally softened into a smile. Her hand came up to clasp Jay's, lacing their fingers together. "Of course not, Harry. We need all the help we can get. And for the record, I think you're right. We should start with Mum Janine, Uncle Bill, and Tom Junior. Patrick and Dad can be next if nothing turns up."

"An excellent idea," Aunt Mimi agreed. "We'll investigate the suspects in tiers, most suspicious to least."

Jay's throat went dry. Even without being told, she knew exactly what *'investigate them'* meant. "Memma, you aren't going to *stalk* them, are you?" she squeaked, letting her hands fall away from Nicole's shoulders. "You're just asking to get arrested!"

"Come on." Nicole turned to give her a sweet smile. "Is it *really* stalking if they're your family members?"

"They're *your* family members, Nicole. How do you think they're going to react if they see me following them? Or Aunt Mimi?" She whirled around to face her aunt, shaking her head in protest. "Lieutenant Slack almost booked you once already. I think that was your only get out of jail free card."

Aunt Mimi sniffed in annoyance. She stood up from her chair, clutching her purse to her chest. "Well then, we'll just have to make sure no one sees us."

Jay's chest tightened, and her heart gave an unpleasant flutter. "What? No, Memma. No! Absolutely not..."

"Good. It's settled then. I'll start tomorrow." Without so much as a goodbye, Aunt Mimi bustled back out into the living room, looking extremely pleased with herself.

Jay held her breath until she heard the front door open and close before letting out a loud sigh of relief. "That was horrifying," she whimpered, resting her chin on top of Nicole's head and closing her eyes. "Please tell me I dreamed that whole thing."

"Sorry, no such luck. But you look like you could use some real sleep, and I should head home anyway." Harry clapped a hand on her back as he passed. "Bye, Vinnie. I'm sure I'll see you around. And Nicky, try not to be too upset about Mom and Dad. You know how they are with death. It's like Tori all over again." He stammered a little over the name, and Jay opened her eyes again. Harry's usual grin was gone, and for a moment, the expression on his face was so lonely that it almost hurt to look at.

Nicole's shoulders stiffened beneath her hands. "I know. Bye, Harry. I'll talk to you tomorrow."

They were suddenly alone, staring silently at the kitchen door. "Wow, you look as miserable as I feel," Jay said at last. She felt stupid as soon as she said it and pulled back, sitting down in the chair next to Nicole. "Sorry. I just..."

"You want to know who Tori is, don't you?" Nicole murmured, meeting her nervous gaze.

Jay nodded. She couldn't help remembering Slack's last interview. The strange expression on Nicole's face when Aunt Mimi had mentioned family secrets. The brief mistake at the party, where Nicole had mentioned that her father had three children instead of two. Even though she didn't have a right to ask, she wanted answers. "She was your sister, wasn't she? You don't have to tell me if you don't want to."

To her surprise, Nicole let out a soft laugh. "Yes, she was. Your Aunt Mimi would be proud of you. Please, don't feel bad for asking. It was going to come up sooner or later. Anyway, I'm the oldest, Harry's the middle child, and Victoria...she was the youngest." Her expression became glassy as she revisited an old memory. "She killed herself two years ago when her fiancé broke off their engagement. It was a horrible shock. All three of us were diagnosed with depression in our teens, but we didn't think she'd actually commit suicide."

For several moments, Jay had no idea what to say. Part of her had known before Nicole said the words, but it was still a shock to hear them. She stared down into her lap, searching for the right response, but eventually, she decided it didn't even exist. There was no right response to a story like that. "That must have been so hard for you," she whispered at last. "Losing your mother and your sister, and now your grandfather. I couldn't imagine that happening to me."

"Thank you for being honest. I usually just get an awkward 'Oh, I'm sorry', and it drives me up the fucking wall. It's even worse when people say 'I understand'. If they actually understood, they would know better than to compare stories." There was a long pause, and she saw tears brimming in Nicole's eyes. "Suicide really is the ultimate sin. The people left behind live with the guilt for the rest of their lives, wondering if they could have changed things."

On instinct, Jay leaned forward and opened her arms. She could offer comfort even if she wasn't any good with words. She pressed a kiss to Nicole's hair and held her tight, rubbing up and down her back. A small wet patch bled through the collar of her blouse, but she didn't care. "I'm sure she never meant to hurt you. She was just scared. Sometimes, when people are really scared..." She hesitated, unsure how much she should share and unwilling to make the conversation about her instead of Nicole. "They think stupid things. They do stupid things...without thinking about how much it might hurt someone else."

Nicole sighed against her shoulder, her voice still tight with tears. "Yeah. Stupid sounds about right. No...I don't really mean that. She wasn't stupid. She was sick and scared, and it wasn't her fault. I know I'm capable of falling down that same dark pit if I forget to take my happy pills. I just wish she'd called me. Or that I'd called her. Something. Maybe I could have helped."

The 'sorry' that Nicole had warned her about rose in her throat, but Jay managed to swallow it down at the last second. There was one other thing she could say, something she knew Nicole would appreciate more. "I'm really grateful for you, Nicky. I'm grateful you're alive, and I'm grateful you're here with me. When you're around, I feel less afraid."

Nicole pulled back, sniffing and running her sleeve over her eyes. But when she lowered her arm, she was smiling. "Thanks, Jay. I'm grateful for you, too."

***

"Oh, fuck me," Jay groaned as Aunt Mimi's car pulled to a stop in the parking lot. She didn't have to ask where they were. Bright neon signs flashed from every angle, burning the name into her brain: *Lucky Winds Casino—Win Big!* She didn't have to ask why they had come here, either. Obviously, they were tailing a member of Nicole's family. She felt sorry for whichever unfortunate soul Aunt Mimi had decided to follow first.

"Language, Jay." Aunt Mimi reached over and pinched the side of her arm. She flinched away, rubbing her shoulder sulkily even though it hadn't really hurt. "Hurry up. I want to make sure we catch him before he leaves."

"He? And who are we stalking today?" As much as Jay wanted to remain in the car and away from the tasteless, faux-Native American decor, she knew better than to leave Aunt Mimi to her own devices. If she did, things would go from bad to worse.

"William Rorsche."

"You mean Nicole's Uncle Bill?"

"Yes." Aunt Mimi swung her fire engine red purse over her shoulder and clicked over toward the casino's front entrance in her heels. "The nervous-looking gentleman with the bad comb over. I learned from a reliable source that he spends a lot of his time here. His gambling addiction isn't exactly a secret to the rest of the family."

"Who's your source?" Jay asked hesitantly, unsure if she really wanted to know.

"Nicole, of course. She's been very forthcoming with information about her family."

Jay couldn't help wondering if her aunt had found out about Victoria, too. She doubted Nicole had mentioned it, but if the story had been in all the papers, Aunt Mimi had probably read about it somewhere during her 'research'. She kept silent as she followed Aunt Mimi through the sliding doors, trudging reluctantly a few paces behind.

"I've already got it all planned out," Aunt Mimi said. They approached the security guard, and she fumbled through her purse for her ID while Jay reached into her back pocket. "We'll start by the slot machines and make our way over to the events area."

She gave Aunt Mimi a suspicious glance. "Just how many times have you been here?"

"Enough." Once the security guard handed her ID back, she started off again, moving through the noisy, crowded room at a fast clip. "Hurry up, Jay. Your lunch break's only an hour."

Jay sighed. She was already going to be late getting back to work. The drive to the casino had taken twenty minutes, and it would take another twenty to get back to the chain bookstore where she worked. "It was supposed to be half an hour." She broke into a jog, but each breath brought in a cloud of foul-smelling smoke, and she ended up coughing into her elbow. Aunt Mimi slowed down and allowed her to catch up. "*Someone* called my boss and said I had to leave early for a family emergency."

Aunt Mimi didn't slow her pace. "I would consider murder an emergency, wouldn't you? Look, there he is," she said, pointing to one of the brightly colored machines.

It was hard to make out the round, hunched figure sitting in front of it, but Jay had to admit that it could have been Nicole's Uncle Bill. He had the same thin, greasy hair, but so did half the other men wandering around. "What are you going to do? Question him?"

Before Aunt Mimi could explain her strategy, someone else approached Bill from the other end of the row. He was tall, beefier than the security guard out front, and much better dressed than the jeans and T-shirts crowd. Jay stared until Aunt Mimi grabbed her shoulder and shoved her in front of the nearest machine. "Play," she ordered, taking the seat next to her.

She looked at the price of each spin and winced. "But—"

"Play! And listen."

Already grieving the loss, Jay withdrew a few precious singles from her wallet and slid them into the machine. Her tips were the only benefit for working half her shifts at the café portion of the bookstore. The lights flashed, and the glowing bear on the edge of the screen roared. She ignored the noise, trying to listen behind her.

"...It's been a month, Bill. Carlo's still waiting for you to pay back that loan."

Jay kept her eyes fixed on the machine, but the nervousness in Bill's voice didn't need an expression to go with it. "Look, I'll have the money soon. I just need a few more wins. I'll play some cards."

"Gambling's what got you into this in the first place. I know you've got the money. You think I don't read the papers?"

"I...I don't know what you're talking about."

There was a sharp banging noise, but Jay didn't dare turn around. *Either the guy slammed his hand against the side of the machine, or...* "What are you afraid of, Bill? Your wife? Trust me, what she'll do to you is nothing compared to what Carlo's capable of. Pay him back, or you'll find out exactly what I'm talking about."

The man stalked away without another word, leaving his shaking, terrified victim behind. Bill followed a few seconds later, scurrying off in the opposite direction and heading for the bathrooms. Jay watched him go, shaking her head in astonishment. The entire scene had been so incredibly surreal that she didn't even feel anxious after witnessing it. "Holy shit. I didn't know things like that happened outside of bad movies."

Aunt Mimi turned to look at her with a smug expression. "It's even more like a movie than you think. The only Carlo I know is Carlo Ritornello."

Jay bit her lip. "The mafia? Really? Aunt Mimi, we live upstate. There are more Amish people here than crime lords."

"Then how do you explain what just happened? I'm sure Bill is capable of driving a couple of hours to New York City. Hmph. And you thought coming here was a bad idea."

"I still think it's a bad idea," Jay muttered. She glanced sadly at her machine. The total read $0.00, and she only had one spin left. With a shrug, she pressed the button and watched the cartoon wheels spin. Bear...bear...red X.

"We were still lucky," Aunt Mimi insisted. She reached down to the bottom of her own machine and withdrew a large string of tickets.

Jay gaped at her in astonishment. "Wait, you were gambling during all of that?"

"Yes. I didn't want to look suspicious." Aunt Mimi smiled and tucked the tickets into her purse. "And I doubled the fifty I put in."

She groaned and rested her head on the machine's cheap plastic surface. "Of course you did," she grumbled as her cheek slid down the side.

"You don't have to sound so sulky about it." Aunt Mimi dragged her out of her seat and toward the cafe. "Come on. I'll buy you lunch, since it is technically your break. And don't make any plans for dinner. Nicole's meeting up with us tonight to do a little more investigating."

Jay sighed and shook her head. There was no way she would be getting back to work on time, and she had a feeling her evening wasn't going to be much better.

Chapter Nine

JAY GLANCED AROUND THE packed club, warily taking in her surroundings. She had been to the city's one and only gay bar a few times—at the insistence of her well-meaning friends—but straight pickup joints were completely alien to her. *This is as bad as the casino,* she thought, trying to ignore the loops her stomach was making. *Noisy. Crowded. Smells like cigarettes and desperation.* Aunt Mimi hadn't told her who they were investigating, but she had a pretty good guess. This was exactly the type of place Tom Junior would frequent. There were plenty of girls and plenty of booze, and her brief interaction with him at the party had made it clear that he liked both.

"Jay! Over here."

She looked up in surprise at the sound of her name, and despite her nervousness, a smile spread across her face. Nicole was wading toward her through the crowd, and she made everyone else fade into the background. Her curls fell messily over her bare shoulders, and her tight black skirt hugged the shape of her hips. Jay whimpered. The longer she looked at Nicole, the lower the thump of the bass traveled in her body. It settled directly between her legs, throbbing in time with the music and Nicole's movements. "Hey," she said, struggling to keep her voice steady.

Nicole laughed. "That's your opening line with me? 'Hey'?"

Jay's stomach did another lurching dive. She felt almost as awkward as she had during their first date. "You're not the type of girl who goes for lines."

One of Nicole's hands wandered around her hip, groping the swell of her backside. "You're right. I go for asses."

She puffed up a bit at the compliment, and she let Nicole's hand stay where it was. "Thanks. You look pretty good yourself."

Nicole arched an eyebrow. "Just good? Try harder."

Jay allowed herself to look a little longer. Nicole's low-cut corset top showed a generous amount of cleavage, and the bottom rode up, revealing a tempting strip of skin at her midriff. Her mouth went dry, and the pounding between her legs grew worse. She suddenly wished her pants weren't so tight. "Sorry. You look fantastic." She touched one of Nicole's silky curls with her fingertips and followed its flowing outline down the side of her throat.

Nicole laughed, staring up at her with sparkling eyes. "That's better. Keep it up and you might just get lucky tonight."

A warm blush crawled down Jay's neck, but the ache that sliced through her abdomen at those words was far more distracting. It had been hard holding back during the first two months of their relationship, but having Nicole around all the time only made things worse. Or perhaps better, depending on how she thought about it. She swallowed, working some moisture into her dry mouth, but she didn't get a chance to speak.

"Look, Jay, I think I see your aunt Mimi." Nicole turned around, standing on tiptoe to see over the much taller crowd. Jay didn't follow her gaze. The sight of Nicole's ass was too distracting. The back of her short skirt lifted higher, offering a teasing glimpse of her thighs. Jay groaned. She was feeling braver than she had in weeks, and part of her wanted to drag Nicole back to the car and run her tongue from the seam of her knee all the way up. Unfortunately, there wasn't enough time. Aunt Mimi was heading straight across the dance floor, pushing aside several young couples as she passed. Most of them turned and stared at her in surprise. She was over twenty years older than almost everyone else in the bar, and with her matching powder-blue purse and shoes, she certainly drew attention.

"Jay, there you are," Aunt Mimi yelled over the booming baseline. "And what are you wearing? I thought I told you to blend in?"

Jay rolled her eyes at the hypocrisy. "I *am* blending in, Aunt Mimi. I think I've passed at least three other people with the same shirt."

"Yes. And all of them were men."

"Leave her alone, Mimi," Nicole said, coming to her defense. "She looks great."

"Maybe in a lesbian bar," Aunt Mimi said with a roll of her eyes. "But she needs to catch Tom Junior's attention."

Any lingering traces of arousal vanished at those words. Jay stared at her aunt in shock, shaking her head and lifting her hands up defensively. "What? No way."

Aunt Mimi ignored her protests. "You don't have to flirt with him.

Just talk to him."

"I thought *you* were going to talk to him."

Aunt Mimi gave her a withering look. "What makes you think he would say anything to me? Nicole's too close, and I'm too old. You're our best shot. He already made a pass at you once before."

Jay started to argue, but Nicole gave her a pleading look. "Please, Jay? I know it's a long shot, but if it helps us figure out who murdered Grandpa, we have to try.

At last, she heaved a sigh. "Fine. What should I ask him?"

"The obvious questions," Aunt Mimi said, shoving her toward the bar. "There. He's sitting on the end. Go!"

"All right, you don't have to shove. I'll go get *one* drink and talk to him. Then, we're going straight home." She headed over to the bar, regretting her decision more and more with each step. "Okay," she said, trying to rekindle some of the courage flirting with Nicole had made her feel. *I can do this, I can do this, I can...oh shit, what am I even doing here?*

Unfortunately, Tom spotted her before she could turn around and disappear back into the crowd. He turned his attention away from the skinny brunette he was chatting up and gave her a long, thorough up-and-down. There was nothing else for it. She couldn't run now. She took the empty seat on his other side despite her disgust. "Hey, Tom."

"Jay? What a surprise. I wasn't expecting to see you again so soon."

The brunette frowned, obviously annoyed by her intrusion. "Who's this?" she asked, narrowing her eyes.

"Nobody important," Tom drawled. "We just need to talk. Why don't you go find your friends and tell them you'll be leaving in a few minutes?"

With a great show of reluctance, the other woman left, casting a few annoyed looks back over her shoulder. Jay pressed her lips together. *Trust me, I'm doing you a favor. This guy's a grade-A creep.*

"So," Tom said, turning back toward her, "does my lovely cousin know you're here?"

Jay nodded. "She's here. I was just getting her a drink."

"And you couldn't resist coming over to visit," he finished for her. "Well, I'm glad."

"Your date didn't seem thrilled about it."

"She'll wait for me. So, what are you and Nicky doing here? This doesn't seem like your type of place. Although I have to admit, you look a lot better than most of the girls here even without showing as much skin."

The compliment made her skin crawl, and she hurried to get the bartender's attention. She almost ordered something strong to make the awkward situation somewhat bearable, but then she remembered Nicole's promise. If they did end up going to bed later, she didn't want to be drunk. "Just a bottle of whatever beer you've got on tap. I'm not picky."

"I'll pay for it," Tom said, raising his hand. "Add it to my tab."

"You don't have to do that," Jay said, but he only shrugged.

"But I want to. I don't think it's a coincidence that you ran in to me here. Why did you track me down? I don't suppose it has anything to do with my late grandfather, does it?"

Jay scooted further away from him, shifting awkwardly in her chair. She barely noticed when the bartender set a bottle in front of her. "Look, Nicole's upset. She agrees with the police and thinks someone killed him."

"Oh?" Tom's eyes didn't give away anything. "And I suppose she thinks that someone might be me. It's not a surprise. I was always her least favorite cousin, and that's saying something, considering Denise's behavior."

"Well, she isn't particularly fond of you."

"I'm not surprised she blames me for this. It's been that way ever since Victoria died. Did you know I'm the one who told Tori's fiancé that she was cheating on him?" Jay gave him a shocked look, but his face didn't twitch. "Oh. I guess she left that part out. That's just like Nicole. She can talk for hours, but never about anything that actually matters."

Jay had to concede Tom Junior's point. Nicole did have a nasty habit of forgetting important pieces of information. Still, she had to come to her girlfriend's defense. "Look," she said, trying to backtrack, "it isn't any of my business."

"Isn't it? By sending you over here, she's practically accusing me. And it's not like I can prove her wrong. Anyone could have slipped that strychnine in his drink." Jay remained silent. "Oh, don't look at me like that. I went in for interviews with the police, too. They told me all about the canister in the garden shed. Thanks to your statement, they think I was trying to sneak some of the poison into the sitting room. I'm their primary suspect."

Jay's stomach sank. "I...I didn't mean..."

"I don't blame you. It's not like I don't have a motive. All that money might tempt anyone into murder. But remember, I'm not the only one. I hear Nicky's inheriting Grandpa's pet project. Lucky girl."

Jay's shoulders stiffened, and she stood up from the bar without touching her drink. "I should go," she said, shoving the stool back and clenching her fists. "Nicole's waiting for me." Her face burned with righteous anger, but guilt churned in her gut. *How does he know what I've been thinking? Okay, he's probably just trying to creep me out or piss me off, but...*

Tom didn't try to stop her. He only gave a casual shrug of his shoulders, resting one elbow against the bar. "Give her a kiss for me, unless you think I'm right. From the look in your eyes, I can tell you have your doubts."

She turned and left without looking back, hating that Tom had been able to get inside her head so easily. His final words kept repeating in her head. *Unless you think I'm right...*

***

When she got back to the place where she had left Nicole, Jay found her staggering under the weight of her very inebriated aunt. Mimi's glasses were askew on her nose, and her purse threatened to fall off her shoulder. "Jayshhhhree," she slurred, tipping a little as Jay rushed forward to steady her.

"Aunt Mimi, what the hell happened to you?"

"Dear God, please take her," Nicole said, shifting some of Mimi's weight into her arms. "I'm not strong enough to keep her upright, and between the accent and the alcohol, I can't understand a damn thing she's saying."

Jay couldn't decide whether to laugh or cry. Her emotions were all jumbled up, and she wasn't sure what to do with them. "I'm sorry about this." She gave Nicole an apologetic look. *And I'm so sorry for ever thinking you could kill your grandfather.*

"It's fine. She's actually kind of funny like this. I just couldn't keep hold of her. She's really strong." Almost at the same moment, Aunt Mimi nearly sent Jay toppling to the ground. She only managed to stay upright with Nicole's help. "Maybe we should get her home. She might hurt herself."

"Or us. How did she manage to get alcohol, anyway?"

"Someone gave her a free glass. They must have mixed in a few shots, because she's totally plastered."

"Nonshense...I'm perflecty...perleft-ly...I'm fineee..." Aunt Mimi insisted, wobbling on her high heels.

"Memma," Jay groaned, still struggling to stop her from toppling over. "You should know better than to drink anything a stranger gives you at a club! *Especially* since the murder we're investigating involves poison."

"Mebbe I'm poishoned," Aunt Mimi said. Her eyes grew wide at the thought. "It'sh in all tha booksh. S'it!"

"This my fault," Nicole said with a wince. "She slipped away from me once you went to talk to Tom Junior. I think she wanted to listen in."

Jay swallowed. She really hoped Aunt Mimi hadn't overheard her conversation with Tom Junior. *The last thing I want is for her to be suspicious of Nicole, too. Maybe she's too drunk to remember...*

"Jayyyyyshreeee. He wasn't. Wasn't telling you everything..."

Or not. She sighed and began hauling Aunt Mimi away, mumbling apologies to everyone she passed. "None of this was your fault," she said to Nicole as they stumbled toward the exit, each supporting one of Aunt Mimi's arms. "She just needs to sleep it off."

"I'll help you get her back to your place. We can set her up on the couch."

Nicole's suggestion left her relieved and disappointed at the same time. Even though she couldn't stop thinking about what Tom had said, part of her had still hoped. *No. It's a bad idea. We shouldn't. It's still too soon.* But each objection she added to her mental list sounded weaker than the last. Her growing feelings for Nicole kept fighting with her fearful suspicions, and she couldn't tell which would win.

Finally, they managed to lead Aunt Mimi through the parking lot and ease her into the back seat of the car. Jay pulled out her keys, holding open the passenger's side door. Nicole's body brushed against hers as she slipped inside, and her muscles tensed. The throbbing was back, and this time, she couldn't blame the music.

"Well?" Nicole asked, staring at her from inside the car. Jay's eyes flicked down to her bare legs, trying not to stare as the hem of her skirt rode up. "Are we going home or what?"

"Yeah. Sorry."

Nicole grinned. "Save it for after we put your aunt to bed. Then you can stare all you want."

Jay swallowed and circled around to the driver's side, still completely confused. As she sat down and buckled her seatbelt, she thought back to her conversation with Tom Junior. *Why do I even care about his opinion? He's a creep, and Nicole hasn't done anything wrong.*

She's one of the nicest, most understanding people I've ever met. Maybe my brain just doesn't want me to have a good thing.

She turned in her seat to see Nicole gazing at her with half-lidded eyes. The affection there made her heart lurch in her chest. If she did this, she knew it wouldn't just be about sex. Not for Nicole, and not for her. It would be a declaration of something deeper. Love. Promises. Trust. Trust she really wanted to give, but wasn't sure she could.

"Jay? Are you okay?"

She shook herself, blinking to clear her head. "Sure. I'm fine." She gave Nicole a soft smile. "Thanks for helping me."

"Are you kidding? Chasing my girlfriend's drunk, mystery-solving aunt around a bar was the best date ever." A loud snore came from the back, and they both laughed. Nicole leaned across the empty gap between their seats, resting a hand on her thigh. Before she could think better of it, Jay leaned in as well, and their lips met in a hot kiss.

All her doubts dissolved as Nicole's mouth slid against hers. Her eyes fluttered shut, and her hands fell away from the steering wheel, reaching out for Nicole's hips instead. She pressed forward, groaning as Nicole's lips parted for her. The strawberry flavor of her lip-gloss added a subtle edge to the sweet, familiar taste of her tongue. At last, they pulled apart, both breathless and beaming.

"Come on, stud," Nicole whispered into her lips. "Let's go back to your place. I think tonight might still be salvageable."

Chapter Ten

"AWW, SHE LOOKS KIND of like you," Nicole said. Aunt Mimi was fast asleep on the couch, snoring away with one arm slung over her face.

"Please don't say that right before we might have sex." Jay slid the strap of Aunt Mimi's shiny handbag from her limp fingers and set it on the floor. Next, she removed the horn-rimmed glasses and tucked them inside. Finally, she grabbed the afghan draped over the couch and tucked it around her aunt's shoulders. "There. She'll be out 'til morning. She's not much of a drinker."

Nicole bumped playfully against her hip. "You sure about that? Because I don't know how quiet I'll be."

Jay's jaw dropped, but Nicole grabbed her hand and dragged her out of the living room before she could speak. They stumbled through the hallway together, laughing and whispering to each other. "Are you sure we should?"

"Definitely. I'm not letting your aunt cock-block me."

"What?" Jay snickered. "Do lesbians even get to say that?"

"This one does. Besides, I bet you've got more than one in your bedside drawer."

"Um." She bit her lip and blushed, reaching up to rub her neck. "Well, about that..."

"Good." Nicole wrapped an arm around her waist, slipping a hand beneath her shirt to skim the small of her back. "But hold that thought, handsome. I've got a few basic tests to run first."

Jay's eyes widened. Her stomach flipped, and as usual, she wasn't sure whether to feel aroused or afraid. Her heart hammered in her throat. "Tests? W...what kind of tests?"

Nicole grinned at her, dragging her into the bedroom by the belt loops of her jeans. "To make sure we're sexually compatible, remember? You've already passed test one." Her face hovered closer, and Jay's hands settled on her hips as their noses brushed.

"What's test one?"

Nicole fisted her hair, dragging her down into a hard, deep kiss. Jay stiffened, then sighed. The only thing that prevented her from melting into a puddle on the floor was her grip on Nicole's waist. She groaned into Nicole's mouth, shuddering as a soft, eager tongue pressed between her lips. By the time Nicole pulled back, she was dizzy and breathless. "So...test one is...?"

"Great kisser. You passed two months ago with flying colors." Nicole tugged on the front of her shirt, placing soft kisses around her mouth as she unfastened each button. Jay tried to catch her lips again, but she drew back at the last moment, hovering just out of reach. "Test number two? Looks good naked."

Jay's breathing came a little heavier. Although Nicole enjoyed parading around in her stolen boxers and little else, she hadn't shown nearly as much skin yet. She didn't have much time to worry as Nicole shoved her shirt back over her shoulders. Goosebumps rose along her arms, but not from the cold. As much as she wanted this to happen, she was still worried something would go wrong. Desperate for something to do with her hands, she unbuckled her belt with trembling fingers and started fumbling with her zipper.

Nicole noticed her panic and took over, brushing her hands aside. "Here," she laughed, "let me." Moments later, her pants slid down to her thighs, and Nicole's palms started running up and down her sides. "God, your skin's so soft...wait." She frowned and glanced down in surprise. "What's this?"

Jay paused in the middle of pulling her undershirt over her head. "What? Oh." She stepped out of reach, turning to show Nicole the orange and black tattoo just above her left hip. "That's my tiger," she said, a little embarrassed.

"You mean Tigger?" Nicole's face broke into a delighted smile, and she let out a soft squeal as she ran her fingers over its outline. "Oh, he's adorable! He looks great on your skin. You're just full of surprises, Jay."

Jay flinched and laughed as Nicole's fingertips ghosted around Tigger's tail. "Hey, that tickles! Stop..." Nicole stopped immediately, and Jay's voice trailed off as she remembered that she was naked except for her underwear. A little of her shyness returned, but to her surprise, she didn't feel afraid. Nervous and awkward, maybe, but not anxious or scared. *I guess I do trust Nicole more than I thought.* "I hope my ink isn't a turn-off. I know my tattoo's a bit...um."

"Subversive?" Nicole teased, raking her nails over the sensitive spot.

"I was gonna say silly, but we can go with subversive. It sounds sexier."

"You're sexy," Nicole purred as she started stripping. Her hips shifted from side to side as she wiggled out of her skirt, and moments later, it flew across the room. Jay swallowed around her tongue, which was suddenly too thick for her mouth. Nicole turned around, offering her back. "Here. Unzip me?"

She took in a shaking breath and obeyed. She brushed aside a curling lock of Nicole's hair and tugged the tab of the zipper down. The corset top peeled apart, revealing several inches of smooth, pale skin. Jay couldn't help herself. She leaned forward, brushing a few wet kisses along the graceful line of Nicole's shoulder. When Nicole hissed and reached back to grab her hips, she summoned her bravery and bit down.

"Oh yessss. You already found the right spot. Harder."

Jay sank her teeth in a little deeper, pushing Nicole's top the rest of the way off before she lost her courage. It fluttered down to the floor and landed at their feet. "You just passed test three," Nicole said, leaning back to whisper beside her cheek. "Follows instructions well."

She released Nicole's shoulder with a soft pop, smiling proudly at the soft purple mark she'd made. "What about test two?"

Nicole turned in her arms, looking her up and down. Her tongue darted out to run across her lower lip. "A-plus."

Jay couldn't help returning the gaze. A heavy throb shot between her legs as she took in the gorgeous sight in front of her. Nicole's dark hair was tossed in a storm around her shoulders. Her lips were full and swollen, cherry red from kisses. Soft brown freckles dusted her skin, and her breasts were capped with tight pink nipples. Jay whimpered and chewed on her lower lip, resisting the temptation to reach out and touch.

Nicole seemed to read her mind. She reached out, taking Jay's hands in hers and cupping them over her breasts. "Go ahead. You don't have to wait for me to boss you around every step of the way."

Jay grinned, running her thumbs around the rapidly hardening points. "Maybe I like it when you're bossy. It's actually kind of hot. And it means I never have to wonder what to do next."

"Really? Good. Because I've got plans for you." One of Nicole's hands slid down along her back, and she yelped when it grabbed a handful of her ass. "Get on the bed. It's time for test four."

Jay didn't bother asking what test four was. Knowing Nicole, she would enjoy it no matter what. She flopped backwards onto the bed, folding her arms behind her head in what she hoped was a casual pose. Her eyes grew even larger as Nicole shimmied out of her panties, dangling them from one finger and flicking them onto her stomach. She stared down at them in shock for several moments, but looked up when the mattress dipped beneath her.

"Well?" Nicole straddled her hips, hovering over her with a confident smirk. "Any thoughts?"

Jay remained speechless. Her gaze trailed along Nicole's stomach, lingering on the subtle curve of her abdomen before traveling between her legs. A neat black strip led the rest of the way down, but her outer lips were completely bare. The slick pink flesh shimmered with wetness, and her folds were already petaled apart. The firm point of her clit peeked out from beneath its hood, and its tip was painted a deep, glistening red.

"I...I...um..." she stammered. She knew she had to say something, but the sight was too much for words.

"You...what? Died and went to heaven? No. You're just really, really lucky." Nicole pounced on top of her, pinning her shoulders to the bed and taking another hard, hungry kiss.

"Bu...but I...unnnfff..." She moaned as Nicole's tongue pushed past her lips. The longer the kiss lasted, the more she couldn't help thinking that air was overrated. "What about...foreplay?"

Nicole broke the string of kisses and beamed down at her. "That's what making out in the car was for. It's time for the next test."

Jay nodded her head, blowing a few strands of Nicole's hair off her face. "Okay. What is it?"

The mattress dipped again as Nicole shifted up. "Test four. Gives awesome head."

Jay's mouth tingled with the promise of salt and sweetness. She had spent the past two months fantasizing about what Nicole would look like. Smell like. Taste like. And even though this wasn't the position she'd had in mind, the more she thought about it, the more appealing it seemed. She ran her hands up along Nicole's sleek thighs, urging her forward. "God, please," she murmured, staring longingly between Nicole's legs. "I...I want..."

Nicole ran a hand down along her stomach, parting her fingers in a v and using them to hold herself open. "Yes?" she said, drawing out the word and waiting expectantly.

Jay's bottom lip trembled, and she swallowed down a whine. Nicole wasn't going to let her get away with anything. "I want to taste you," she said at last, too eager to care how she sounded.

"Not bad," Nicole said, giving her a broad smile and a nod of approval. "We'll work on your begging later." She finally lowered her hips, and Jay lifted her head off the pillow, meeting her halfway.

Nicole tasted even better than she imagined. All warm honey, just heavy enough to fill her mouth without being overwhelming. Her selfishness got the better of her, and she ran her tongue over every inch of flesh she could reach, eager for more. Nicole allowed it for a little while, but her patience didn't last long. Her hands shot down, and Jay whimpered as they gripped the back of her head. "My clit could use a little attention," she purred, directing her to the right place with a gentle tug.

A pounding ache shot down between her legs at the order. She followed Nicole's guidance, shifting up until she found the straining bud of her clit. It was already swollen, and it fit perfectly between her lips as she pulled it inside. She flicked over the tip, softly at first, then harder when Nicole's hips rocked forward. Nicole let out a deep, satisfied sigh and stroked the side of her cheek in encouragement. "Mmhmm, just like that."

The praise made her even more determined. She tightened her grip on Nicole's thighs, desperate for something to hold. Heat ran down along her chin, and she groaned around her prize as the motions above her sped up. Nicole's hand slid around the back of her head, raking through her short hair and holding her in place. "Not fair. You weren't supposed to make me come this fast."

The thought of making Nicole come made Jay's head spin. It was all she wanted, all she could think about. She dove into her task, following the thrusts of Nicole's hips and sliding a hand between their bodies. She waited to make sure her touch was welcome, but Nicole gave her an answer almost immediately. "God, yes. Inside. Hard."

She found Nicole's entrance with two fingers, pushing past the outer ring of muscle. Tight, clinging heat clamped down around her, and Nicole's clit throbbed at the same time. Even more wetness slipped over her chin, and she could feel the shallow, rippling pulses that came between. Nicole was close, and she knew it would only take one more push.

"Forward. Angle your fingers like..." Nicole let go of her head and shifted on top of her, causing her fingertips to scrape against a swollen spot along her front wall. The new pressure earned a shout, and Jay looked up along Nicole's body in awe. Her breasts bounced with each push of her hips, and her stomach tensed as her inner muscles pulled impossibly tight. "Oh, Jay!"

The sound of her name made Jay's chest swell with happiness. She lashed her tongue one last time and hooked her fingers forward. Warmth rushed into her hand, splashing up to cover her mouth and chin. She gasped against the flood, catching as much as she could while the tight bundle of Nicole's clit twitched in the seal of her lips.

At last, the shivering stopped. Nicole gazed down at her with sparkling eyes, panting as she shifted her hips back. "Is there a grade higher than A-plus? Because you earned it." It took Jay a few moments to find her words. She reached up to wipe her mouth with the back of her hand, stalling for time, but Nicole caught her wrist. "Don't. I want to kiss you first."

Jay didn't even have time to be surprised as Nicole dragged her forward again. It was hard to kiss when her lips kept threatening to split in a smile, but somehow, she managed it. Finally, they broke apart, and both of them started laughing at the same time. "Wow," Jay said, trying to stifle her giggles. "I wasn't expecting that, but...Damn."

"I did warn you that I was a power bottom on our third date," she teased. "I had a feeling you wouldn't mind some assertiveness. But it's my turn now."

Her eyes widened. "Again? I mean, I don't mind, but..."

"No, silly. I mean it's my turn to get you off. I might be a little bossy in bed, but it doesn't mean I'm selfish."

"Just in bed?" Jay quipped before she could stop herself.

Nicole rolled her eyes and gave her a gentle cuff on the side of the head. "You ass. Spread your legs and lift your hips. I can't believe I forgot to take your boxers off before."

She obeyed, arching off the mattress as Nicole settled between her thighs. She blushed when she realized that the cotton was completely soaked through, and from the look on Nicole's face, she had noticed, too. "Well, that's a bonus," Nicole said, glancing at the dark wet patch for a moment before tossing her boxers aside. "I have a feeling this won't take long."

Jay shivered. "Don't tease me," she groaned as a soft mouth began skimming up the side of her thigh. "I...I don't think I can handle it after..."

Nicole nipped a soft place above her knee. "Don't worry, I won't. Not this time, anyway. You already look pretty desperate." Jay's cheeks flushed, but she didn't have time to be embarrassed. Nicole's mouth travelled higher, and she cried to the ceiling at the first swipe of her tongue.

There was no warm-up. The blissful heat seemed to be everywhere at once, sliding between her lips, closing around her clit, pushing inside of her. The sensations were so intense that she couldn't separate them out. They melted together until all she could feel was a single burning glide. She rocked forward, unsure whether she was straining toward release or running away from it. "Fuck, Nicky..."

Nicole pulled away, pressing a few lingering kisses to the tip of her clit. "That's a promising response," she laughed, bringing up the tips of her fingers to replace her mouth. "I must be doing something right."

Jay gave Nicole a pleading look. She tried to beg, but she was beyond words. She could barely remember her own name. The pounding fullness inside of her was unbearable, and her breath came in short, sharp gasps. She spread her legs wider, muscles clenching as Nicole's fingers traced back and forth.

Thankfully, Nicole didn't draw out her torment. She dipped forward again, sucking hard at the shaft of her clit and pushing forward with her hand at the same time. Jay stiffened at the stretch, and a sob tore from her throat. She thrashed as the warmth pulled even tighter around her, clenching down hard when Nicole's fingers slid over the perfect spot.

Unable to stand it anymore, she looked down and met Nicole's eyes. What she found there almost stopped her heart. *How could I have doubted?* The love and affection written on Nicole's face was obvious even though they hadn't shared the words. Warmth rolled through her entire body, and her release finally hit. She shivered and spilled over, clutching the sheets as she screamed.

Somewhere between contractions, Nicole's mouth moved down to her entrance. The fingers inside of her pulled back, but a firm tongue replaced them, pushing forward and coaxing out a fresh burst of wetness. Her clit pulsed until Nicole's slick fingertips started rolling over it, and she surrendered, shuddering with each pass. She tumbled through wave after wave, lost to the rest of the world.

Even after her peak faded, Jay remained flat on her back for several moments, too exhausted to move. Her head flopped sideways on the pillow, and she sank back into the bed, still trembling with aftershocks. "Holy shit," she breathed, blinking the blurriness from the edges of her vision. "You're incredible. What did I do to deserve you?"

"Everything," Nicole said, scooting up to rest against her stomach. "And for what it's worth, you passed the last test."

"Oh?" Jay's eyebrows lifted. "What's the last test?"

Nicole began tracing patterns around the dip of her navel, and it took Jay a moment to realize she was drawing a heart. "You made me feel something. We weren't just having sex." To her surprise, Nicole's expression turned nervous. "At least, I hope we weren't just having sex."

Jay's grin filled her face as she slung one of her arms over Nicole's back. "No. We weren't just having sex."

Nicole breathed a sigh of relief. "Good. Now, flip me over. It's your turn to be on top."

Chapter Eleven

THE NEXT MORNING, JAY woke to the smell of food, the warmth of Nicole's body curled against hers, and the horrifying sight of Aunt Mimi's horn-rimmed glasses. She cried out in surprise, yanking the sheets up to her nose. "Memma! What are you doing?"

Aunt Mimi barely seemed to notice her embarrassment. "Good morning! Here, eat your breakfast." She held out a plate, and Jay stared in disbelief.

"Masala dosa? How long have you been up?" That question led to others, and a flush spread across her face. *If Aunt Mimi woke up sometime during the night to start making the batter, she might have...*

"A while," Aunt Mimi said. "You know I'm a light sleeper."

Jay groaned and refused to take the plate. "Great," she mumbled, throwing an arm over her eyes. Maybe if she kept them closed long enough, Aunt Mimi would disappear and she could wake up all over again. The last thing she wanted to think about was what her aunt might have overheard.

Unfortunately, the still form next to her began to stir. "Hey," Nicole breathed, slinging an arm around her waist and cuddling closer. "Are you awake alre...Oh, shit."

Jay sighed. Apparently Nicole had finally noticed their unwelcome guest. "I'm sorry," she groaned, sliding further under the comforter until it almost covered her head. "I didn't think she'd..."

"Make breakfast?" Aunt Mimi interrupted cheerfully. "I don't mind at all. I thought you two might need it."

To Jay's surprise, Nicole tucked the sheets beneath her arms and shifted into a sitting position. "Did you say breakfast? That smells great. What is it?"

"Masala dosa. Think of a thin pancake stuffed with spicy potatoes and onions."

"Stuffed pancakes? Potatoes? I'm in. Thanks."

Nicole pulled the plate onto her lap, and Jay sighed. There would be no getting rid of Aunt Mimi now. "Later, we're going to have a long talk about personal boundaries," she mumbled.

"I won't be staying long," Aunt Mimi said, ignoring her completely. "I just wanted to feed you before I go back home. Tinkerbelle needs to be let out soon."

"Tinkewbew?" Nicole said around a mouthful of food. She swallowed and tried again. "Do you have a pet?"

"Yes. Tinkerbelle's a miniature poodle."

"No it's not," Jay muttered under her breath. She loved dogs, but Tinkerbelle was the meanest canine she had ever encountered. "That thing might look like a poodle, but it's pure evil."

Nicole gave her a curious look, but Aunt Mimi didn't give her a chance to ask questions. "She won Best in Show at her last competition. I'm trying to breed her, but the stud prices are ridiculous. In my opinion, they should be paying me..."

Jay zoned out as Aunt Mimi kept talking. Her eyes slid over to the plate in Nicole's lap, and her stomach rumbled. As much as she hated to admit it, she wanted the food. "Pass it over, please," she said at last, sulking a little as Nicole offered her the plate. She shoved a forkful in her mouth and swallowed hastily.

"...and that's why I think we should follow your stepmother next."

Jay's eyes widened, and she nearly choked on her next bite. "Wait, back up. How did the conversation go from Tinkerbelle to mystery solving?"

Aunt Mimi gave her an exasperated look. "Weren't you paying attention? I was talking about taking Tinkerbelle to the groomer, and Nicole said..."

"Mum Janine has a hair appointment today," Nicole said. "Mimi could drop by."

"No." Jay folded her arms stubbornly over her chest. "Absolutely not. Trailing someone to a casino or a bar is bad enough, but a hair salon? That's way too much like stalking."

"It's not stalking if we have a good reason," Aunt Mimi protested. "Besides, she's one of the most likely suspects. With Stephen Fox out of the way, her husband inherits the family business, and her stepdaughter inherits the Fox Foundation."

Jay turned to look at Nicole. "You don't actually think she did it, do you?"

Nicole shrugged. "I don't know what I believe. I'm kind of hoping if we talk to Mum Janine, we can prove she's innocent and Tom Junior's guilty. My stepmom and I don't always get along, but I'd rather send him to prison than her."

The worried crease in the middle of Nicole's forehead wore through Jay's resolve. "Fine. But I'm just sitting in the lobby. She already hates me after that awful dinner."

"Good," Aunt Mimi said. "I'll pick you up on your lunch break. You can watch Tinkerbelle while I get my hair done."

Jay flopped back onto the bed and stared at the ceiling. *What the hell did I just agree to?*

***

Jay hunched her shoulders, trying to ignore the growls coming from behind her. "Can't we stop at your house first?" she asked, shooting a nervous glance at the back seat. The depths of Tinkerbelle's cage fell into shadow, but she could make out the poodle's evil, glowing eyes in the dark. "I'm not sure a hair salon is the best place for a dog."

"Nonsense," Aunt Mimi said. She had replaced her horn-rimmed frames with prescription sunglasses and wrapped her hair and shoulders in a leopard-print scarf. Of course, the shoes and purse matched. "I'm sure an upper-crust establishment like *François* caters to celebrities with animals all the time." She screeched to a stop, almost ramming the front bumper into the curb. Tinkerbelle snarled again, and Jay's stomach lurched.

"We live upstate, Aunt Mimi. There aren't any celebrities here."

"Wealthy socialites, then. Do you think they'd turn Janine Fox away if she wanted to bring her dog?"

Jay tucked her chin against her chest and sighed. She unfastened her seatbelt, slinking out of the car. "I'll go see if they actually take walk-ins," she sighed, praying the answer would be no.

Before she could escape, Aunt Mimi reached out to grab her shoulder. "Wait, get Tinkerbelle. She'll have to stay with you while I get my hair done."

Jay pulled a face. The only thing worse than baby-sitting Aunt Mimi was baby-sitting her dog. "We're just going to end up at the emergency room again," she grumbled, throwing open the back door. She stared nervously at Tinkerbelle's carrier, and the sides rattled as she drew closer. Although the poodle had never actually bitten her, it was the cause of multiple accidents, many of which had required stitches and prescriptions for Percocet.

"Hurry up, she won't bite," Aunt Mimi said, shoving her between the shoulder blades. "She likes you."

"Liar." Jay turned the cage toward her. Tinkerbelle's black lips peeled back over her teeth, but they remained clenched shut instead of snapping. "Easy, pup," she said, trying to hide the nervous shake in her voice. Reluctantly, she opened the carrier door. Tinkerbelle lunged, trying to streak past her, but she managed to block the way. She scooped up the dog and held its squirming body against her chest until it finally calmed down.

"There, see?" Aunt Mimi said, beaming at her as she wrestled with the beast. "I told you everything would be fine. You're a good girl, aren't you, Tinkerbelle?"

Jay pulled a face, but didn't answer. Somehow, she managed to haul Tinkerbelle toward the front door of the salon. "Come on," she huffed, wincing as its claws dug through her shirt. "Let's get this over with."

Together, they stepped into the hair salon. It was wide and spacious, with lots of clean white surfaces and tall mirrors to reflect the light pouring in through the windows. A receptionist sat behind the front desk, and she spotted Tinkerbelle almost immediately. "Excuse me, ma'am, but I'm afraid we don't allow...oh, is that a poodle?"

"Yes," Jay said, almost hopefully. Her anxiety was increasing by the second, and holding a writhing dog in her arms definitely wasn't helping. "Sorry. I can just wait outside. In fact, I'll go do that right now."

Unfortunately, Tinkerbelle seemed to enjoy the attention. Her fuzzy face softened, and her tongue lolled from the side of her mouth as the receptionist reached out to pet her. "No, she's so cute! I'm sure the owner will let her stay."

Jay's heart sank. Of course Tinkerbelle had chosen precisely the wrong moment to make friends. "Uh, okay. Thanks, I guess." She stepped aside and let Aunt Mimi take her place to speak with the receptionist. While they chatted and cooed over Tinkerbelle, she craned her neck, trying to see past the display of expensive, organic shampoos.

"...And I have to use a special body wash for her fur, because her skin is so sensitive."

She wasn't sure whether to be disappointed or pleased when she caught sight of Janine Fox in one of the chairs. She was already halfway through her color, trapped and helpless until the dye finished setting. Jay almost felt sorry for her. Even though Nicole's stepmother didn't seem to like her, it wasn't fair to subject anyone to Aunt Mimi's questioning when there was no escape.

"Why don't you take a seat in one of the chairs over there?" the receptionist asked. "Pick whichever one you like, and someone will be with you shortly."

Jay chewed on her lip as Aunt Mimi stepped behind the desk and chose the chair directly next to Janine. She looked up immediately, and her eyes narrowed with recognition. "What are you doing here?" Her voice was so low that Jay had to lean closer to make it out. "I thought I made it clear that I didn't want to be interrogated about my father-in-law."

Aunt Mimi only smiled. "I'm not here to interrogate anyone," she said, unwinding her spotted scarf and sitting in one of the chairs. "I just need a touch-up."

"I've never seen you here before," Janine said. Her frown carved a deep groove in her otherwise smooth face.

Jay slumped down in one of the waiting room chairs with Tinkerbelle on her lap. She hadn't thought it was possible to regret this trip more than she had in the parking lot. Apparently, she had been wrong. She shot Janine an apologetic look, but the other woman didn't appear to notice.

"We must be on different schedules," Aunt Mimi said. She removed her sunglasses and tucked them into her leopard print purse. "That color looks lovely on you, by the way."

Janine's expression didn't change, but she gave a tiny nod of thanks. She turned to face the mirror, ending the conversation without a word.

The silence seemed to stretch forever. Jay shifted awkwardly in her seat, wilting under the reflection of Janine's hard glare. Her fingers were so desperate for something to do that she started scratching Tinkerbelle's ears. The dog let out a soft growl, and she removed her hand immediately. A battered copy of the *Tribune* rested just out of reach, but she didn't bother getting up for it when she saw the front-page story. Stephen Fox's face was printed beneath the headline.

A loud buzzing noise finally broke the awkward stillness. At first, Jay thought it was her phone, but when she pulled it from her pocket, the screen was blank. Janine checked her purse next, sighing as she answered the call. "Hello?" she said, holding her phone several inches from her hair. A voice spoke on the other end, but the words were muffled. "No, this is his wife. I handle Gregory's appointments."

Aunt Mimi grinned at her over Janine's shoulder and gave her a thumbs-up. Jay stared determinedly down at her shoes.

"What do you mean you aren't releasing them? That's against the law." Another pause. "No, I'm afraid I don't understand." Janine's voice grew slightly louder, and her frown faltered. "What exactly are you implying, Mr. Matheson? That I...Yes. Fine. We'll be there tomorrow. And don't speak like this in front of my children, or we'll find different representation." She hung up the phone without a goodbye and turned her chair around, facing the receptionist. "Excuse me? My scalp's starting to burn. I think I'm ready for a rinse."

The receptionist nodded. "Of course. I'll get Francois. One moment."

Jay froze as Janine rounded on her next. "If you don't mind, I'd like you to give a message to Nicole." Although the words were polite, her voice was full of ice. "Her grandfather's lawyers want to see us tomorrow. She'll know where to go. And please, keep your aunt away. This is family business."

"That's a funny way of putting it," Aunt Mimi said. "From what I've read in the papers, your family's had more than its fair share of bad fortune."

Janine whipped her head back, causing the foil in her hair to crinkle. "What happened to my first husband is none of your business."

Jay could only watch in horror as a familiar, intense look crossed Aunt Mimi's face. "Your husband? I was talking about your youngest stepdaughter. Were you married before?"

Jay stood up, hitching Tinkerbelle underneath her trembling arm and preparing to intervene. "Memma, please don't," she begged, but the words were barely audible. She just couldn't put any force behind them. Her shivering was getting worse, and no matter how fast she breathed, she couldn't suck in enough air to make her lungs stop burning. *Shit shit shit, please not now. Not here. Anywhere but here...*

Janine didn't notice her distress. All her anger was focused on Mimi. "Don't confront me with things you don't even understand. Richard died of a heart attack, Victoria hung herself, and I was devastated. There, is that what you wanted to hear? Does it help your stupid investigation?"

Aunt Mimi remained outwardly calm, but the angrier Janine got, the brighter her eyes became. She started asking questions immediately. "How many years ago? Were you there when your husband—"

Janine left the chair and rose to her full height. "Enough. I don't owe you any explanations about my family." She pulled out her phone, brandishing it like a weapon. "Leave now, or I'll call my lawyers."

"But—"

Jay panicked. She reached forward, trying to get Aunt Mimi's attention and drag her out of the salon. At the same moment, Tinkerbelle saw her chance for freedom. She wriggled free and sprang at Janine, almost knocking her backwards. Jay grabbed for her, but it was too late. Tinkerbelle scrambled up the front of Janine's smock and leapt onto the counter beneath the mirror. She knocked aside combs and curlers, barking angrily at all three of them.

Several people came running from the back of the salon. The receptionist clapped her hands over her mouth, and an angry man with a pink collared shirt started shouting at them. Jay didn't stop to listen. She snatched up the growling Tinkerbelle as fast as she could and grabbed Aunt Mimi's arm with her other hand, hauling them both toward the front door.

"Jay? What are you doing? Let go of me," Aunt Mimi spluttered, trying to head back for her chair. Tinkerbelle thrashed under Jay's arm and added to the noise, barking as she tried to leap down to the floor. "I was just about to ask—"

Aunt Mimi was strong, but she was stronger. With a force of will she didn't know she possessed, Jay managed to drag both her aunt and Tinkerbelle out of the salon before Janine or the screaming man reached them. Several hair stylists watched them go in shock, but she didn't care. The ache in her chest was building and building, and tears blurred her vision. "This has to stop. What part of lawyers didn't you hear? If you keep bothering Janine, she'll sic them on you," she shouted, her voice rising in pitch.

"But Jay, don't you want—"

"All I want is for you to leave my girlfriend's family alone! This isn't one of your stupid books, okay? In the real world, we have trained professionals to deal with things like this, and *you* are *definitely* not one of them. Because of you, my entire fucking life is a mess!" She shoved Tinkerbelle into Aunt Mimi's arms and scowled at the wet, foul-smelling stain seeping down the front of her shirt. "Great, just what I need. Take your stupid dog and go. Now."

Shock and hurt crossed Aunt Mimi's face, but the expressions barely even registered in Jay's mind. The sick thud of her heart drowned everything else out. "Muthey, please, let me help..." Jay didn't answer.

She couldn't. She threw one arm out blindly, trying to shove Aunt Mimi away. Then she stumbled through the parking lot, desperately looking for a place to curl up and hide.

She found one in a small park half a block away. Thanks to the cold, it was mostly abandoned. She curled up on a rickety wooden bench tucked beneath a tree, folding her arms on top of her knees and using them to hide her face. She tried to calm her breathing, but it hurt too much to pull the air deep. She could only manage shallow inhales between her chattering teeth, and her entire body started to shake.

This isn't happening right now. This isn't happening. I'm fine. I'm making it all up. This isn't real...

The tears swimming in her eyes spilled free with sharp, hitching sobs. She couldn't control them, and soon, her sleeves were soaked. *Shit. I look so stupid. I sound so stupid. And all these words keep running through my head but I can't get my fucking mouth to say them and now I'm crying all over myself and why am I such a total fucking mess?*

For the next several minutes, she couldn't get her body to do anything. The logical part of her brain struggled to cut through the overwhelming fog of fear, but she couldn't obey its commands. One moment, she tried to move her arms, screaming inwardly at herself when her muscles wouldn't respond. The next, she was too terrified to do anything. *Oh my god I can't stop what if I never stop what if I die I'm going to die like this on this stupid fucking park bench and then everyone will think I was completely crazy because I died from a fucking anxiety attack fucking goddamn shit.*

After a while, the string of profanities in her head led into slower, less labored breaths. Still shivering, Jay tried to move her arms again. They wouldn't leave her knees, but she was able to grasp her pants with her twitching fingers. The grip helped. She inhaled again, and the burning wasn't as bad.

"Shit," she groaned, managing to say it aloud. She burst into manic, relieved laughter even though she felt completely empty and hollow inside. "My shirt. My fucking shirt is completely ruined. Tinkerbelle pissed on it and I cried all over it." She slumped over in exhaustion, still laughing as the cold wind dried the tear-lines streaked across her cheeks. Her anxiety attacks usually ended this way, in a state of exhausted disbelief where the least-funny things imaginable suddenly seemed hilarious.

Eventually, the laughter died out. She swallowed the lump in her throat, ignoring her creeping sense of guilt as she lowered her feet back to the ground. "I was right," she whispered as she untied her jacket from around her waist and slipped it on. She didn't care if it got ruined, too. She was dead freezing. "I might feel like I'm going crazy half the time, but I know I'm right. Aunt Mimi has no business hurting other people that way." She pulled out her phone, trying to decide whether she felt normal enough to call for a cab. *But if I'm right, why do I feel so lousy?*

Chapter Twelve

JAY GROANED IN FRUSTRATION and tugged at the uncomfortable shirt she was wearing. It was too tight around her shoulders, and the material itched, but at least it wasn't covered in dog piss. She was lucky her manager kept a spare change of clothes back in the office. The rest of the workday had gone fine despite her breakdown. A severe anxiety attack usually left her too damn tired to be afraid, and she went through the motions of her job in a state of numbness, grateful not to feel much of anything.

Once again, she debated stopping back at her apartment to change before visiting Lieutenant Slack, but there wasn't much point. The station was right on the way home, and it seemed stupid to make two trips just because she hated her shirt.

She hesitated outside the door, staring up at the sign and chewing on the inside of her cheek. Fighting with Aunt Mimi was inevitable, but reporting her to the police felt like a step too far. She had only been trying to help. *Yeah, help get herself arrested. And don't get me started on how bad she's made me look in front of Nicole's parents.*

But that was the crux of the problem. *Am I really here to keep Aunt Mimi out of trouble, or am I out for revenge?* She sighed and fixed her sleeve again, wincing as it cut into her bicep. *That's me. The lamest superhero ever. About to rip through my shirt and go crying to the police for help with my nutty aunt. Besides, I have other people to think about. Nicole...*

She smiled a little as her thoughts returned to the night before. For a few hours, before everything fell to shit, her life had seemed perfect. Her fears and doubts had been blissfully silent, and she felt more connected to Nicole than ever. That was enough to make up her mind. Nicole wanted to be with her now, but that could change if Aunt Mimi pissed off the entire Fox family. She didn't want their relationship to end just when it was starting to get serious.

At last, Jay squared her shoulders and stepped inside. She approached the front desk, giving the woman a small wave as she signed in. She took a chair by the window, resting her hands on her knees to keep them from jumping. She still had no idea what she was going to say.

She didn't get much time to think about it. Slack arrived less than a minute later with Bellows at his side. His eyes widened in surprise when he saw her, but the bags underneath them still made his blunt face look worn and tired. "Miss Vinkatessin, what are you doing here?" he asked as he led her down the hall. "Most people don't come to the police station just for a visit."

Jay shrugged. "It's not my favorite place. I wouldn't have come, except my crazy aunt is getting crazier than usual."

"The lady with the weird handbags, right?" Bellows asked. Slack silenced him with a glare as they entered the interrogation room.

"Yeah, that's her." Jay didn't bother sitting down, but she set her shoulder bag on top of the table and rested her hand on the nearest chair. "I have a couple of things to tell you. The first is that my aunt has started following people."

Slack snorted in exasperation. "Huh. Of course she is. A crazy wanna-be detective stalking suspects is just what this case needs. It's not like every reporter on the planet isn't already bothering them."

"I'm concerned. If one of the Foxes calls you, just get her away from them before they bring in their lawyers."

"You want us to arrest her?" Bellows asked in surprise.

Her stomach twisted. "I don't know. Just do what you have to do. But call me if you actually throw her in jail." She gave the two officers a sheepish look. "She drives me crazy, but we're family."

"Hopefully it won't come to that," said Slack. "My boss already thinks the investigation is a train wreck. And to be honest, he's probably right."

"Maybe I can help," she offered. "I did find out a few interesting things while I was trying to keep my aunt out of trouble. Nicole's Uncle Bill is in serious debt to some guy named Carlo. We think he's the head of the Ritornello family."

Slack raised his eyebrows. "We think? So, you've been following people around too?"

"I've been doing damage control," Jay said. Normally, the accusation would have upset her, but her emotions were still too flat to respond. "I can leave if you don't want to hear what I found out."

"No, I want to hear it," Slack said. He folded his arms across his chest, waiting expectantly.

"Bill's got a gambling problem, and he doesn't want his wife to know. If she inherits, he can pay off his debts."

"Wouldn't she notice the missing money?"

Jay thought back to her only conversation with Nicole's long-winded, hypochondriac Aunt Martha. "His wife's not the brightest bulb in the box. He could get away with it."

Slack did not look convinced. "Sure, he's got a motive, but so does everyone else."

"That's not the only thing we found out. Tom Junior has hurt someone before."

That got Slack's attention. "Hurt someone how?"

"Indirectly. He provoked his cousin Victoria into killing herself a couple of years ago." She shuddered. "I knew he was a creep the first time we met."

"Suicide isn't exactly murder," Slack pointed out.

"But isn't it strange that no one else brought it up during the interviews?" Bellows asked.

"Why would they? Their goal is to make themselves look good so the police don't keep investigating and cause a scandal. They've already got reporters nosing up their asses, not to mention this one's crazy aunt." Slack jerked his thumb in her direction. "Rehashing old family drama doesn't look good for anyone."

"There's one more thing," Jay added in a soft voice. She took in a deep breath through her nose. Of the three suspects they had tailed, Nicole loved Janine the most. If it turned out to be her, she would be devastated. "Janine Fox was married once before. Her husband died from a heart attack."

Slack narrowed his eyes. "Let me guess. It was under mysterious circumstances?" Jay nodded. She didn't need to say anything else. "All right. We'll look into it. Anything else?"

Jay shook her head. "No. That's it. Um, give me a call if you run into my aunt." She grabbed her bag, squeezing past Slack's bulky frame to escape through the door.

It was easy to find her way back to the front entrance. "I've been spending too much time here," she muttered to herself. "I can't believe I have the station's layout memorized."

It was barely past six, but the sun was already gone from the sky. She shoved her hands in her pockets and scanned the parking lot, trying to remember where she had parked her car. To her surprise, she wasn't alone. Another figure was heading for the station, and the closer he came, the more familiar he looked. Her stomach clenched when she caught sight of his face. Tom Junior was heading straight for her.

At first, Jay worried that he had followed her. Her heart hammered faster, and her stomach twisted. But as she continued watching Tom Junior, she realized that he wasn't paying attention to her at all. He kept glancing back nervously over his shoulder, a gesture that seemed almost uncharacteristic. Her first instinct was to head toward her car without confronting him. *This is a bad idea,* her mind screamed even as her feet started moving without her permission. *Last time, he actually made me wonder if Nicole had killed her grandfather.*

Tom finally noticed her. He turned in surprise, and Jay thought she caught a flash of fear on his face before his usual smug smile took its place. "Miss Venkatesan. We just seem to run into each other everywhere, don't we?"

Jay pressed her lips together. She was already regretting this confrontation. It reminded her of something Aunt Mimi would do. But she couldn't stop now. "Funny, isn't it? So, what are you doing here?"

"What else? I'm under suspicion for murder. Is it so surprising that I want to check in with the police?"

She gave him a long look. "Yeah. It is."

"I'm not as heartless as Nicole thinks." The flash of nervousness reappeared. "Have you thought anymore about what I told you?" She clenched her teeth. "You don't have to tell me. I know the answer already."

"No, you don't," Jay snapped. Her fingers clenched into a trembling fist around the strap of her bag. "I don't know all your ugly family history, and I don't get why you have such a big problem with Nicole, but I don't care. I trust her. She didn't do anything wrong."

Tom's irritating smugness returned. His lips curled in an unfriendly, insincere smile. "If you trust her so much, why are you here talking to me? You know it makes logical sense. Nicole always wanted control of the Fox Foundation, and she always hated me. The old man was going to die anyway. Why not take care of both of us at the same time? Kill him, and blame me for it. You weren't with her the whole evening. She could have put the strychnine in his drink before you and I came back to the sitting room. Then, all she had to do was leave it in the shed for the police to find. I get arrested, and she has everything she wants."

Jay felt like she had been punched in the gut. Hearing Tom strip her own thoughts bare was a sickening invasion. She thought back, remembering every single moment she had spent with Nicole, analyzing their interactions. *No, Tom couldn't be right. Nicole loves me. I saw it in her eyes the night before and felt it in her touch.*

"Think about it. She didn't tell you the whole story about Victoria, did she? She hasn't told you a damn thing about what our family's really like. And you're still stupid enough to trust her."

"You're a hateful piece of shit," Jay snarled, turning away from him in disgust.

"Wait—" He reached out to grab her arm, but she yanked free of his grip.

"Let go of me! I'm tired of this. Leave both of us alone, or I'll go back into the station and report you to Lieutenant Slack."

Tom took a step back, holding his hands up in mock surrender. "Fine, fine. But don't say I didn't warn you. This is all going to unravel, and you're going to be sorry you didn't get out when you had the chance." He hurried past her, giving her a wide berth as he headed for the station.

Jay shivered and wrapped her arms around herself, sniffing against the cold. She stood alone in the middle of the empty parking lot, too stunned to head for her car. Tears stung her eyes, but they weren't just tears of anger. She felt even guiltier than before. Tom was awful, but she was worse. All he had done was give voice to the thoughts that lived in the very back of her mind. She hated herself even more than she hated him.

***

Nicole was waiting for her when she finally arrived back at the apartment. Once again, she was naked except for a pair of stolen boxers and a revealing tank top. The sight of her smile made Jay's chest ache as she stepped through the door. "Hey you. You're home later than I thought. How'd it go with Mum Janine today? Did you make it to the salon?"

She cut off the barrage of questions by raising her hand. Once she kicked off her shoes, she sank down onto the couch and reached for the spare afghan. "I don't want to talk about it," she sighed as she tucked it around her legs.

Nicole shifted closer to her on the couch, cuddling against her side. "It's up to you. You're allowed to have bad days sometimes. God knows

I've had plenty since Grandpa died...You aren't still mad at your Aunt Mimi for this morning, are you? I thought it was sweet of her to bring us breakfast in bed, even if it was really embarrassing."

Jay shook her head. "No, I'm not mad at her for this morning. We got into another fight later. She was harassing your stepmother, so I told her to get lost."

"Really?" The look on Nicole's face was somewhere between pride and disapproval. "Don't get me wrong. I'm impressed you stood up to her, but was she that awful? I know she's a handful..."

"She stepped out of line," Jay said. "She basically accused Janine of murdering her first husband." She hesitated, propping herself up further on the couch's armrest. "Did you know about that? Maybe tell the police during your interview?"

"Of course I did. I love Mum Janine, but if she did kill Grandpa, I want the truth to come out."

"What about Tom Junior? Did you tell them he was the one who made Victoria kill herself?"

Nicole remained silent for a long moment. She swallowed, and the color left her cheeks. When she spoke, her lips trembled around the words. "Did he tell you that at the bar the other night?" Jay nodded. "Well, it's not true. He's an alcoholic, Jay. Victoria confronted him over it, so he lied to her fiancé and made up some story about her being unfaithful. But that doesn't mean he killed her. Normal people don't react to a broken engagement by hanging themselves in their wedding dress." Nicole's voice cracked, and a few tears leaked from her eyes. "Tori committed suicide because she had a severe mental illness. Not because of Tom."

Jay didn't answer. She rolled onto her back and spread her knees, making room for Nicole to lie back against her chest. The weight and warmth of her lover's body was comforting, but the knot in her stomach pulled tighter. "It wasn't because of you either," she said after a while. She stroked her palm up and down along Nicole's bare arm, trying to soothe her quiet sobs. "You know that, right?"

Nicole leaned back against her shoulder and wiped away a few stray tears. "Yeah. I know. But she was family. I should have been there for her."

Another stab of guilt almost made Jay flinch. Her emotions had picked a really inconvenient time to come flooding back. She was starting to feel awful for the way she had treated Aunt Mimi, and even worse for the terrible things she had assumed about Nicole. She pressed a kiss to Nicole's temple, inhaling the scent of strawberries that clung to her hair and trying to shove her feelings down for just a little while longer. Nicole needed empathy right now, not for her to turn into a sloppy mess. "Your sister knew you loved her. She knows."

"Promise me you'll make up with your Aunt Mimi, okay?" Nicole asked softly. "I know she isn't a suicide risk, but you never know when someone you love is going to die. You don't want to wonder about what could have happened."

"All right. I'll apologize to her once I've had a little time to cool off." That reminded Jay of her promise to Janine. "Wait, I almost forgot. Your stepmom wants the whole family to talk to your grandpa's lawyers tomorrow afternoon."

Nicole turned to look at her. "Will you come with me? Please, Jay. I don't want to be alone with my family right now. You've been way more supportive than any of them lately. I know I can trust you."

Although she hadn't really been as supportive as Nicole thought, Jay couldn't resist the pleading look in her girlfriend's eyes. "Okay. But don't be surprised if your stepmom flips out when she sees me. We didn't leave things on the best of terms since Tinkerbelle attacked her."

"Wait," Nicole laughed, "Aunt Mimi's poodle attacked Mum Janine? What happened? No one got hurt, right?"

"That wasn't the worst part," Jay said sadly. "Here, I'll tell you. If I don't, I guess you'll hear about it from someone else sooner or later."

Chapter Thirteen

THE LAW OFFICES OF Brenner, Matheson, and Associates were designed to impress. Jay whistled as she and Nicole crossed the first floor on the way to the spacious glass elevator. It looked more like a modern version of the palace of Versailles than a waiting room. "Wow," she whispered, letting go of Nicole's hand and rubbing the back of her neck. "I didn't know lawyers had fountains and paintings in their lobbies. Are you sure I should be here?"

"You're here because I want you to be." They stopped in front of the elevator, and Nicole turned to face her. "Please, Jay, I need you right now. This is the first time my entire family's been together since Grandpa died."

The sadness in Nicole's eyes made Jay's insides squirm. She sighed, pressed the button, and reached for Nicole's hand again. "Okay. But the last time I saw your stepmother, Tinkerbelle was peeing on both of us. I doubt she'll be thrilled to see me."

Nicole squeezed her fingers tighter. "I don't care what she thinks."

"Don't care what who thinks?" Jay turned to see Harry crossing the lobby toward them. "Going up? I think we're on the seventh floor."

"Don't care what Mum Janine thinks, and yes, that's right."

Nicole opened her arms for a hug, and Harry gave her one, picking her up and twirling her around. Jay smiled at the sight. *At least I'm not Nicole's only support system.*

"What's Mom's problem?" Harry asked as he set her down.

Jay coughed in embarrassment. "Uh...well, I—um, the other day..."

Nicole jumped in to save her from floundering. "Jay's dog attacked her at the hair salon yesterday."

"Excuse me. That *thing* is not my dog."

"Or I guess Jay's aunt Mimi attacked her. She flipped out and threatened to lawyer up."

Harry snickered in amusement. "I might have paid money to see that. She's usually sickeningly polite to everyone. What did your aunt say to get her so angry?"

"I don't know. At first I thought she was mad about Victoria…" Harry flinched at the mention of his sister, and Jay quickly moved on. "But then she started talking about her first husband. I didn't quite understand."

Nicole shrugged. "There's not much to understand. Mum Janine hardly ever mentions Richard to us, and she talks about Victoria even less. I don't think I've heard her say Tori's name since the two of us cleaned out her apartment. I had to take all the photo albums because she could barely look at them. She doesn't handle death well."

"That would be an understatement," Harry sighed. Thankfully the elevator arrived, cutting off the depressing line of conversation. They entered together and waited as the doors closed. "So, has your aunt figured out whodunit yet?" He leaned past her to push the button for the top floor. "I'll admit, I haven't found out anything new."

Jay tapped one foot nervously as the lift started to rise. She shoved her hands in her coat pockets for protection, but hooked her elbow through Nicole's first. "If she knows, she hasn't told me. We're kind of not speaking right now."

"Why not?"

"Because of the dog incident," Nicole explained. "Come on, Harry, let's not talk about this right now."

Harry leaned against the metal railing on the side of the wall. "But isn't that why we're here, Nic? To talk about it?"

"We're here so they can tell us why they aren't releasing Grandpa's money. That's it." Jay was a little surprised by Nicole's change of heart. Before, she had seemed almost eager to help Aunt Mimi solve the mystery. Maybe Nicole was finally going to listen to her and let the police handle things. *Or maybe she doesn't want the mystery solved…* She frowned and shook herself, squashing those thoughts down. She didn't want to be like Tom Junior. Trust was a choice, and it was a choice she wanted to make. *No. Stop it. That's my anxiety and Tom Junior talking. Nicole's been nothing but wonderful.*

When the elevator arrived at the seventh floor, she kept her arm looped through Nicole's instead of pulling back. Her heart sank when she saw that the rest of the family was already there. Tom Junior was slouched in his chair, looking pale and exhausted, but his bloodshot eyes darted toward her. Uncle Bill withdrew a handkerchief from his pocket and rubbed it over his sweaty forehead. Janine's appearance was flawless, and she aimed a sharp glare at them as they exited the lift.

"What is she doing here, Nicole?"

"She's here for me." Nicole's face hardened, and she seemed to fill the room despite her short height. "Everyone else brought their partners."

"Everyone else is married and they haven't been *stalking* our family."

Jay wanted to curl in on herself and hide, but Nicole didn't budge. "For now, Jay's a part of this family. If you want to be mad at her aunt, that's fine, but don't blame her. I need her here today."

Janine opened her mouth to continue arguing, but Harry jumped to her defense. "Come on, Mom. She won't go to the papers if that's what you're worried about."

"That isn't what I'm worried about."

Awkward silence fell over the room. Nicole led her to one of the empty seats, and she slumped into it, avoiding Janine's eyes. Unfortunately, someone else caught them instead. Nicole's cousin Denise was sitting on her other side, staring at her curiously. Her bubblegum pink lips matched her outfit, and her fancy bag was almost as strange as one of Aunt Mimi's. "I don't mind that you're here. I like any woman who can rock short hair."

Jay ran a self-conscious hand through her hair. Maybe Denise wasn't so awful after all. "Uh...thanks?"

"So, do you have any tattoos?"

"Um, I have one of a tiger," she said, shifting awkwardly in her chair. Nicole flashed her a small smile and squeezed the top of her thigh.

"Where? Can I see it?"

"She'd have to take off her pants, Denise," Nicole said. Denise giggled, and Janine shot her another angry look.

Fortunately, a lawyer in a sharp suit chose that moment to come out of his office. "Good afternoon, everyone. I'm Mr. Matheson, and I'm here to go over a few details with you concerning Stephen Fox's estate."

"Bullshit," Tom Junior said. "You're here to tell us you aren't giving us our inheritance."

There were a few gasps and murmurs from the group, but Mr. Matheson ignored them. "It's not that simple. If you'll all come with me to my office, I'll explain further." He gave Jay a look, and she sank lower in her chair. She usually moved through mostly-white spaces without much of a problem, but in this situation, she stuck out like a sore thumb.

It was obvious that she wasn't part of the Fox family.

"She stays with me," Nicole insisted, speaking before anyone else had the chance to object to her presence.

Mr. Matheson waited, but when no one else objected out loud, he shrugged his shoulders. "All right. Shall we?"

As a group, they got up and followed the lawyer into his large, plush office. There were several couches and chairs positioned in front of the desk, and everyone quickly found new seats. Jay made sure to position herself on the end of the furthest couch. Nicole sat on her other side, acting as a shield between her and the rest of the family.

"So, I assume you all know why you're here," Mr. Matheson said. He circled behind his desk and withdrew a thick file from one of the drawers.

"I have no idea," said Aunt Martha. She gave an exaggerated sigh. "I hope it's important, because I had to cancel a doctor's appointment to come. My heart—"

"You don't want to give us the money," Tom Junior said before Martha could get started.

That stopped Aunt Martha's tirade. For once, the chatty woman could find nothing to say.

"I wouldn't put it that way," said Mr. Matheson.

Nicole's father crossed his arms over his broad chest. "Stop talking like a lawyer. If you aren't releasing the money to us, we deserve to know why."

"Don't be stupid, Uncle Greg. It's because one of us killed him," Tom Junior said. Beatrice gave him a warning glance, but he ignored her. "Come on, you can say it. We're all thinking it."

Mr. Matheson adjusted his glasses. "We're putting a temporary hold on all payouts until the matter of Stephen Fox's death has been resolved. We are not accusing anyone. As the executors of his will, we simply want to be sure that his estate can be divided correctly."

Tom leaned forward, putting his elbows on his knees. "What you're really saying is that if one of us is convicted, we won't get a cent."

"You can't hold it," Uncle Bill blurted out. He withdrew his handkerchief and started mopping his face again. "The will is clear. That money is ours!"

"Why do you need it so fast?" Tom Junior asked. "So you can pay off your gambling debts?"

Everyone gasped. "Beatrice, say something to your son," Aunt Martha shouted. Her face flushed almost as red as Uncle Bill's and her eyes nearly bulged out of her head. "He just accused my husband of gambling and associating with a crime family."

Beatrice shrugged. She seemed twitchy and distracted without a drink in her hand. "If you want to shut him up yourself, be my guest. Tom and I can't do a damn thing with him."

"If you won't deal with him, I will," Janine said. She turned in her seat to face Tom Junior. "You've been nothing but disrespectful since your grandfather died. Why he included you in his will, I have no idea, but if you don't stop drinking, you won't live long enough to enjoy it."

Tom's face twisted up. "Oh, like you don't have your own dirty little secrets. We all know about your first husband. Didn't take you long to find a rich second one, did it? Have the police questioned you about dear old Richard's heart attack yet?"

"Stop it, all of you," Harry shouted. He left his seat, and his hands bunched into fists as he towered over the rest of the group. Everyone quieted down, and even Tom stared at him in shock. "This isn't the time. We're here to talk about the will." He turned to Mr. Matheson. "Are you legally allowed to freeze our grandfather's assets like that?"

"Not permanently, no, but we are allowed to launch an investigation. Not in to the murder itself, but into Mr. Fox's finances."

Tom Junior rolled his eyes. "In other words, you want to bury it in paperwork until you're sure a huge chunk of the trust fund isn't going to a murderer. The press would rip you apart. Good luck finding clients after that."

Nicole glared at him. "You didn't have to say it like that."

Tom Junior glared back. "It's the truth."

"It is the truth," Matheson admitted. "This is the safest possible thing to do, considering the circumstances."

"You do realize," Janine said, her voice icy cold, "that you're accusing a member of this family of murder?"

"I'm trying to protect my firm, Mrs. Fox. If no one is guilty, then there will be no problems, and everyone will get their money."

"When, exactly?" Uncle Bill's face dripped with sweat even in the air-conditioned office.

"That depends on how quickly this business is resolved."

Tom Junior gave a careless shrug of his shoulders. "If I drink myself to death by the time I'm fifty five that still gives me a good thirty years to enjoy my inheritance. Do whatever you want."

"Don't talk about death like that," Nicole snapped. Jay felt her stiffen, and she looked like she was about to join Harry in the middle of the room. "Despite what you think, it's not some big joke."

"Don't pretend we're still talking about our grandfather," Tom Junior said, torn between anger and fear. "I know you want me framed for this. You've always hated me, ever since Victoria..."

"Don't say her name." Fresh pain tightened Harry's face, and he began blinking rapidly, as if forcing back tears. "Sorry, Mr. Matheson, I'm leaving. If there are any more details I need to know, just tell Nicky." He pushed open the door and left the rest of the group staring after him, too surprised to say anything.

To Jay's surprise, it was Patrick who broke the stunned silence that followed. He gave Tom Junior a look of utter disgust. "Sometimes I wish you weren't my brother. There was no reason to bring Victoria in to this."

"I think you should leave, Tom," Nicole said in a shaking voice. "None of us want you here."

Tom Junior pushed back his chair and stood up, although much more slowly than Harry. "That works out perfectly, because I don't want to be here. But maybe you should ask your girlfriend about our conversation last night. I'm not the only one who thinks you're guilty." He followed Harry out of the room, and the bottom dropped out of Jay's stomach.

Oh shit.

Nicole turned to look at her, but Jay avoided her eyes. She couldn't find the courage to look into them. She began to shake, and a lance of panicked pain pierced her chest.

"I think we're done here," said Mr. Matheson, but to Jay's ears, his voice sounded all washed out. "Our representatives will be in touch with you regarding the will's status and execution."

"Come on, Jay. Let's go." Nicole took her hand, leading her out of the office. The grip was uncomfortably tight, but Jay didn't try to pull back. Her head was clouded with fear. She had no idea what she was going to say. What she could say. *Shit, shit, shit. She can't know I was thinking those awful things about her. She'll never forgive me. I'm worthless...*

"I don't believe him," Jay blurted out as they stepped back into the elevator.

Nicole dropped her hand and jabbed at the button for the first floor. "But you did before. You thought I killed him." Her voice broke with emotion, and Jay's stomach lurched at the look of utter betrayal on her face. "How could you? I thought you trusted me."

"I do," Jay said. "I...I didn't say anything..."

"You didn't have to. I saw the look on your face. You stayed with me, comforted me, *slept* with me, and all along, you thought I was a murderer!" She tried to reach out, but Nicole stepped back, pressing against the wall to avoid her. "Don't. Don't touch me. So, when did you change your mind? Was it when you realized every word that comes out of Tom Junior's mouth is a lie, or was it after we fucked? You sure didn't seem to be afraid of me then."

Jay fumbled for words, but nothing came out right. Her throat ached, and her teeth wanted to chatter. "I—it wasn't like that..."

"Then what was it, Jay? I stood up for you in there. I did it because you were there for me. Because you acted like you loved me the way I love you. But the whole time, you were thinking horrible things about me." She sniffed and swiped her sleeve across her eyes, but Jay saw the tears streaming down her face. They were coming too fast to hide. "Get your own ride home. I don't want you anywhere near me right now." The elevator doors opened, and Nicole stormed out.

"Nicole, wait," she shouted, but it wasn't enough. Nicole left through the front doors, not even turning at the sound of her name. Jay sank down onto one of the benches by the fountain and buried her face in her hands. Her tears came seconds later, seeping through her fingers as her body shook with uncontrollable sobs. Like her trust, they had come too late to do any good.

Chapter Fourteen

JAY BURIED HER FACE in her pillowcase, trying to slow down her breathing. After her breakdown at Mr. Matheson's office, she had returned to her apartment and locked herself in her room. Two anxiety attacks in two days should have left her too tired to feel anything else, but her body hadn't gotten the memo. The past several hours were a blur, and she was still a mess. The bands of muscle around her chest ached from overuse, and her eyes were sore from crying.

In her lucid moments, she tried to think of a way to apologize to Nicole, but it seemed useless. Nothing she said would take back her betrayal. *I deserve this.* She huddled deeper under the covers. *Why do I have to ruin every good thing that happens to me? I should have trusted her...*

Should have. There were too many should-haves for her to keep track of. She should have told Nicole about her conversation with Tom Junior. She should have brought up her doubts so Nicole could reassure her instead of hiding them. She should have reached out for help instead of trying to deal with her fear alone. She should have been the supportive girlfriend Nicole had thought she was.

Girlfriend...there was no way she was still Nicole's girlfriend now. Their relationship had ended as soon as Nicole ran out of the elevator. The thought almost sent her into a tailspin again, especially since Nicole had called her part of the family just a few minutes earlier.

"I hate this," she sobbed into her pillow, her voice muffled by the fabric. *No, you fucking coward. You hate yourself.*

She needed to talk to someone. Family, a friend, anyone. But her family wouldn't understand, and she didn't have many friends. She hung out with co-workers and the girls on her softball team from time to time, but none of them knew her well enough to accept nighttime phone calls and listen to her problems. She had fallen out of touch with several of them over the past few months while she spent more and more time with Nicole.

Nicole. Nicole had changed something fundamental in her. For the first time in her life, she had felt like someone was listening. Like someone heard her. She had never believed in stupid things like soul mates, but if that wasn't love, she didn't know what was. Now, that chance was gone, unless…unless she could get Nicole back. She had spent hours feeling sorry for herself, but Nicole was the one who really needed comfort and an apology. The thought made Jay feel sick all over again, not from guilt, but with a sadness she couldn't describe. She needed to fix this. Not so she could feel better, but because she hated the thought of Nicole hurting.

Jay rolled onto her side and glanced over at the neon red light of her digital clock. It was 1:00 in the morning. If she showed up at Nicole's house now, she would definitely be told to fuck off. And she would deserve it. But there was one place she could go. One person who hadn't abandoned her. One person who always put up with her mistakes, even though she also made plenty of her own.

"Shit. I guess I have two apologies to make."

She pushed herself out of bed with a low groan and stumbled toward the bathroom, rubbing her eyes. If she was going to Aunt Mimi's house, she needed a shower first.

***

Jay regretted ringing the bell as soon as she pressed the button. Loud, frantic barking started almost immediately, and something slammed against the front door. She flinched, jumping back in surprise and almost tripping down the steps. The mangy mutt was obviously just as mean in the middle of the night as she was during the day.

A few moments later, the door opened. Jay watched warily as Tinkerbelle streaked out through the open door, but luckily, the dog didn't lunge for her legs. Instead, she ran out on to the grass and squatted near some bushes. Swallowing with relief, Jay turned back around to face the house. Aunt Mimi was waiting in the doorway, staring at her expectantly. "Well?"

"I'm an idiot," Jay said, folding her hands behind her back and hanging her head. She hadn't thought there was room in her heart for any more awful feelings, but facing Aunt Mimi made her feel even worse than before. Nicole wasn't the only person she had let down.

The toe of Aunt Mimi's bright purple shoe tapped on the porch.

"And?"

Her shoulders slumped. "And you were right. About everything. I thought you were embarrassing me, but really, I embarrassed myself. I'm so sorry."

A warm hand reached out to touch her shoulder, and she looked up. Aunt Mimi's eyes were smiling behind her horn-rimmed glasses. "It's okay, muthey," she said, holding out her arms. "I forgive you. And maybe I overdid it a bit, too. I should have seen how upset you were. Questioning a suspect isn't worth hurting my favorite niece."

Jay stepped into the hug, tucking her chin over her aunt's head and holding her close for several moments. Her eyes stung, but the knot in her chest loosened a little. They stayed that way for a long minute until Tinkerbelle ran over to nip at her shoelace. Jay groaned, trying to nudge her back without kicking.

"Tinkerbelle, bad girl." Aunt Mimi bent down and hooked her fingers through Tinkerbelle's collar, dragging her back inside. "Come in, Jayshree. I'll make you something."

For once, she didn't object to the use of her full name. "It's fine, Memma. You don't have to feed me every time I come over."

"I have rice cakes."

"Done."

They entered the house together, and Jay trailed into the kitchen on Aunt Mimi's heels. "So, why are you really here? It can't be just to apologize. I knew you'd get around to it eventually."

"Eventually?" Jay's eyebrows rose in surprise.

Aunt Mimi headed over to the pantry and began removing sealed containers. "Of course. You're a good girl, and you always apologize for your mistakes. But I was expecting it to take a couple more days, and happen at a more reasonable hour. Why now, at two in the morning?"

Jay sat down at the kitchen table, winding her ankles around the chair legs. "I ruined things with Nicole," she mumbled. There was silence as Aunt Mimi waited for her to continue, and the edges of her lips twitched up in a sad smile. Maybe Nicole wasn't the only person who actually cared enough to listen after all. "She found out I'd been talking to Tom Junior...and that I thought she might have killed her grandpa."

Aunt Mimi clicked her tongue in disapproval. "Oh, Jay. I know I said 'everyone's a suspect', but that was for me, not you. My job is to figure out who killed Stephen Fox. Your job is to support Nicole through her loss."

"Well, I know that *now*. I couldn't help it. You know what my brain does with horrible thoughts."

"And did you tell Nicole this?"

"Well, no… She knows I have an anxiety disorder, but that's about it. I try really hard not to let it affect her." Jay chewed on her lip as Aunt Mimi set a plate down in front of her. The sight of the speckled white rice cakes made her stomach growl despite her guilt. She broke off a piece and shoved it into her mouth, moaning at the familiar taste. Aunt Mimi made the best comfort food in the family.

"Why? It affects you. Don't you think your feelings are important enough for her to know about?"

Jay swallowed, taking a moment to think about her answer. "I was scared, I guess. It's a lot to put on someone else early in a relationship. And then when it started getting bad, I was afraid she'd think it was an excuse. What was I supposed to say? 'Hey, honey, I know you're still in mourning, but my stupid brain keeps imagining that you killed your grandfather. But I know you probably didn't, I'm just a nutcase.'"

"Well, I wouldn't put it quite like that, but it's a start. Nicole's a sweet girl. I don't think you're giving her enough credit."

Jay sighed. Once again, Aunt Mimi was right. Sure, Nicole occasionally fudged the truth, but she was also unquestionably accepting. Nicole had accepted her quietness, her nervous tics, her mumbling and social awkwardness. She had even accepted Aunt Mimi's eccentric behavior without a single negative comment.

Tiny claws scrabbled across the kitchen floor, and Jay looked down to see Tinkerbelle sitting at her feet, staring up at her with pleading eyes. "Go away," she groaned, nudging the dog with her foot. "This is people food."

"She can have a bite."

Hoping it would be taken as a gesture of peace, Jay broke off another bite of the rice cake and threw it onto the floor. Tinkerbelle gobbled it up at once, and the pompom at the tip of her tail started wagging. "No wonder she's always so mean. You have her in that ridiculous poodle cut."

Tinkerbelle glared up at her as if she understood, tiny black eyes glinting under the doggy-afro piled on top of her head. Jay felt a small pang of sympathy until Tinkerbelle started whimpering for more food. "Ugh. If I can convince Nicole to take me back, I want us to get a big, friendly golden retriever or a black lab."

"Nonsense." Aunt Mimi sat in the other chair, carrying a steaming cup of tea in her hands. "Poodles are wonderful dogs. You can have a pup from Tinkerbelle's next litter."

She shuddered at the mere idea. "Get her spayed, Memma," she pleaded. "I don't want to think about any of Tinkerbelle's spawn running around, especially in my apartment."

"Spay a prize-winning show dog? Never." Aunt Mimi took a long sip from her cup. "But you're avoiding the subject. Have you tried talking to Nicole since the fight? An explanation and an apology probably wouldn't hurt your chances."

Jay shook her head. "No. She seemed pretty mad. Tom Junior was an ass at the meeting with Mr. Fox's lawyers, so she was already close to tears before we even started fighting."

"Really? Why?"

"He brought up Victoria. It's a sensitive subject for her. Did you know she and Harry were the ones who found her body? She hung herself in her wedding dress. Nicole cried in my arms when she told me." A lump formed in Jay's throat as she remembered some of their previous conversations. The sadness mixed with relief in Nicole's voice. The way she smiled after she cried. The way her body relaxed afterward, as if she had shrugged off a great weight. They had been a perfect fit. Or would have been, if she hadn't ruined everything. "It must have taken a lot of trust for her to tell me. Ever since the party, she's made a huge effort to be open and honest. And I repaid that trust by being a total dumbass. My heart knew it wasn't her, but my stupid brain wouldn't shut up."

"The first step to fixing this is admitting you were wrong. You know what the second step is, right?"

"Well, I think I need to help you solve the mystery. If we figure out who killed Nicole's grandfather, maybe she'll forgive me for being so monumentally stupid."

"Solving the mystery won't fix this. You need to apologize before we catch the murderer. She's angry and upset because you didn't trust her the way you pretended to. You need to prove that you do. Now, before we have a name to give the police."

Jay pushed her plate away, tossing the last bite of rice cake down for Tinkerbelle to devour. Suddenly, she wasn't hungry anymore. "But what do I say? I feel more lost than ever."

Aunt Mimi reached across the table to squeeze her hand. "Just tell her everything you told me...with a little something extra to prove you mean it. I think you already know what you have to say."

The suggestion sent a fluttery feeling through Jay's chest. Part of it was fear, but something else stirred underneath, something warm and comforting. Maybe it was what she had been afraid of all along, but she couldn't for the life of her remember why. The feeling seemed—right.

"So, what? I just show up at her house and tell her I love her? She'll probably think I'm crazy."

"Crazy in a good way," Aunt Mimi insisted. "You have to be the one to reach out. If she loves you back, she'll listen. Love is about forgiveness, just like I forgave you."

Jay sighed. Aunt Mimi was right again. As always. She stood up from the table and straightened her shoulders. "Okay. But if she calls the police, you have to come bail me out. You owe me one, remember?"

Aunt Mimi smiled and stood up from the table, pulling her into another hug. "After this, I'd say we're even. Go get your girlfriend back."

Chapter Fifteen

IT WAS STILL SEVERAL hours before sunrise by the time Jay reached Nicole's house. All the windows were dark, and starlight winked down at her as she stepped out of the car. She huddled deeper inside her jacket, clasping her phone with cold fingers and hoping she would feel it buzz. Nicole hadn't responded to any of her texts yet, but she didn't want to give up. Not until she apologized the right way.

The walkway seemed longer than usual as she headed for the front door. The lawn was covered in shimmering frost, and her breath spun upwards in silvery trails as she trotted up the steps. She shifted from foot to foot once she arrived on the porch, debating whether to use the doorbell or call first. Eventually, she decided to ring the bell. Nicole could silence her phone, but it would be harder to ignore her physical presence.

A chime echoed through the house, and Jay rocked back on her heels, waiting in silence. Part of her didn't expect Nicole to open the door, but then a light switched on above her, and she heard footsteps coming from inside. "Nicole, it's me." She caught a glimpse of Nicole's face in one of the windows beside the door, but it swiftly moved out of sight. "I only want to talk for a minute."

The door opened. Nicole's eyes were red and puffy from crying, and her face was blotchy around the edges. She had an afghan draped around her shoulders like a cape, but underneath, Jay could just make out an old pair of her boxers. "Why are you here? It's three in the morning. I don't want to talk."

"Then just listen." Nicole started to object, but Jay gave her a pleading look. "Please?"

Nicole sighed, folding the afghan tighter around her shoulders. "Fine. You have one minute."

Jay took a deep breath. She didn't need one minute. She only needed a second. "I love you."

Nicole's lower lip trembled, and she inhaled sharply. "W…what?" For once, she had been struck speechless.

"I love you."

Nicole let out a hoarse laugh, clearly still in shock. "That's not fair. You don't get to come here and say that to me."

"Please, let me finish." Jay paused, but Nicole didn't order her to leave. Even though her heart was breaking, she couldn't help but smile. It felt like she had been waiting forever to say these words. "I love you, Nicole Fox. So much. I should have chased after you the second you left that elevator, but I'm an idiot."

"Obviously," Nicole said, but the roll of her eyes wasn't convincing.

"Letting you go was the dumbest thing I've ever done. I know you, Nicky. You would never hurt anyone, especially your grandpa. You kept saying I was your rock during this mess, but really, you've been mine since we met. I'm sorry I was too stupid to tell you before now. And I am so, so sorry I didn't make it clear that I trust you."

"Why? If you love me, why didn't you trust me?"

"I do trust you. My brain just does stupid things without my permission." It was an incredibly inarticulate way to explain it, but she barreled on, determined to do her best. "Sometimes, these awful thoughts pop up and I can't get rid of them. It's like getting a song stuck in your head. You don't want it there, but it keeps coming back."

A little of the hurt disappeared from Nicole's face. Instead, she looked thoughtful. "Does this have anything to do with your anxiety?"

Jay nodded. "It kind of feels like a cop-out to pin all the blame there, but yeah. They're related."

"You should have told me sooner," Nicole said. "I would have understood. I know what it's like to have awful thoughts you can't get rid of. Depression, remember? I could have told you how stupid and crazy you were being, and we could have laughed and moved on." She closed her eyes, letting out a long silver stream of breath into the cold air. "Do you know what I've been thinking all this time, Jay?"

Jay chewed on her lip. "I don't know. How much of an idiot I am?"

"Not quite. I've been going back over my actions, all the lies of omission. I kept wondering what I'd done to make you believe I was a murderer. You've spent the past two weeks taking care of me, and it hurt to think you were just pretending the whole time."

"No," Jay blurted out. The last thing she wanted was for Nicole to blame herself. "This wasn't your fault at all. I mean, yeah, you should have warned me about your family, and you should have told me who you were, but you've been really honest with me since then. You didn't have to tell me about your sister. You didn't have to stand up for me in front of your family. You listen to me. You hold my hand whenever I have to talk to a stranger because you know how nervous I get. I *never* really believed you could kill someone, no matter what my stupid brain was screaming. The truth is, I don't deserve someone like you. Someone smart, kind, beautiful..."

"You forgot rich and way out of your league," Nicole teased.

Jay felt some of the weight lift from her shoulders. If Nicole was joking with her again, maybe that meant things would be okay. "Yeah, and way out of my league." She pulled her hands out of her pockets and held them out in hope. "Please...forgive me?"

Nicole didn't take her hands. Instead, she folded an arm around her neck and pulled her close. The kiss was soft, but firm enough to make her shudder. A wave of guilt crashed over her, but she couldn't bear to move away. There was something else behind it, something that threatened to swallow her up—love. And this time, she wasn't afraid to put a name to it. They parted at the same time, sharing nervous glances. Jay's cheeks flushed. It was like their first kiss all over again. In some ways, it was.

"Hey you," Nicole said with a shaking breath. "I love you back. I forgive you. But only if you forgive me, too. I should have known better than to listen to Tom Junior, of all people, and I shouldn't have run out on you while you were falling apart. You deserved a chance to explain."

"I was so stupid," Jay whispered against Nicole's lips. "And scared, and—"

"Don't be scared." The afghan pulled tighter around both of them, and Jay could feel Nicole's heart thumping as fast as hers. "I want to hear the rest of your apology again. The first part."

"I love you." Something broke inside her, and she couldn't stop repeating it. "I love you, I love you," she murmured, pressing butterfly kisses to Nicole's hair, her cheeks, her forehead, the corner of her mouth.

"You'd better, because I'm already crazy in love with you. And I don't do love half way." She closed her eyes, and Jay kissed the lids.

Jay felt like she had been saving her kisses for a lifetime just to give them to Nicole. She didn't want to hold any of them back. They stayed on the front porch for a long time, holding each other close. Neither of them wanted to move until a gust of wind blew through the open door, startling them both.

"You should come in," Nicole said, backing out of her arms. "It's freezing out here."

Jay kicked the door shut. "Worth it."

"I'm glad you think I'm worth standing out in the cold for. So..." A smile spread across Nicole's face, and Jay was thrilled to see that her color had returned to normal, although her cheeks were still a rosy pink. "Are we going to have make-up sex or what?"

Jay stared at her in surprise. Her lips moved soundlessly as she tried to come up with a response. "...What? Sex? Us?"

Nicole's hands slid lower, and Jay squeaked in surprise when they cupped her ass. "Do you see any other hot women standing around in my house? Yes, sex, us. So get ready. You've got a lot of apologizing to do."

"Okay." Her face broke into a wide grin, and she moved to take off her coat, but Nicole caught her before she could head for the stairs. "Wait, what are you..." She was cut off with another kiss. Nicole dropped the afghan onto the floor, dragging her down along with it. Jay's fingers flew to Nicole's shoulders, hanging on for dear life. The weight of what she had almost lost crashed over her, but she felt relief instead of guilt. She wanted to remind herself that this was real with her hands, her lips, with every shared breath.

Nicole seemed to understand. Instead of surging over and taking control, she rolled onto her side, bracing her weight on one elbow. Her lips curved into an indulgent smile, and her soft eyes seemed to say, *go ahead.* It was an invitation Jay couldn't resist. She let out a grateful sigh as she nuzzled Nicole's neck, relearning the taste of her skin. Even though they had only been together once before, she remembered each detail—the salt, the sweetness, the warmth. Her hands shook as she eased away the straps of Nicole's tank top, kissing the faint indents they had left behind. "How did I get so lucky?" she murmured against Nicole's collarbone.

One of Nicole's arms draped around the back of her neck, fingertips tracing the column of her spine. "How did *we* get so lucky?"

That gave her even more confidence. Jay slipped one of her hands beneath Nicole's tank top, running over the smooth, flat surface of her stomach. "You really think you're lucky to have me? Even after all this?"

Nicole nodded. "Yes. Absolutely."

After that, there was no more need for words. Jay pulled Nicole's tank top over her head, kissing along the slope of her chest. Her palms roamed along Nicole's sides, stroking up from the swell of her hips all the way to the widest part of her ribs. The tips of Nicole's breasts were already pebbled and hard, and she drew one into her mouth, circling it with her tongue.

A gasp hitched in Nicole's throat. She rocked forward, and Jay shuddered as warmth pressed against her stomach. Her own shirt had ridden up, and she could feel heat burning through the pair of boxers Nicole had stolen from her. Suddenly, she wanted them out of the way. She needed to feel every inch of Nicole's flesh against hers without any barriers left between them.

Nicole's boxers slid down with one soft tug. Jay's jeans came next, although kicking out of them was a little more difficult. While she fumbled with her zipper, Nicole took care of her shirt, drawing it up and off. As one, they both seemed to realize they were naked. Jay froze, staring at Nicole with a mixture of shyness and amazement. Their first time had been playful, but their second time threatened to steal a piece of her heart. She smiled. As long as Nicole was holding on to it, she didn't want it back.

The next several moments bled together. One kiss became a string that travelled back and forth. Their legs tangled. Finally, Nicole's hand clasped hers, guiding her fingers lower. She groaned as the tips found wetness, but Nicole swallowed the sound with her mouth. Her hips pushed up, and Jay stopped worrying. This was exactly where she was supposed to be.

Jay took her time exploring, making a careful study of Nicole's reactions. She experimented until she found a stroke that earned soft sighs, and continued adding pressure until they became whimpers. Each new discovery thrilled her, but the sounds weren't enough. She needed to give more. To show Nicole she was worthy of trust. To share the love that threatened to burst from her chest.

Once again, Nicole seemed to know what she wanted before she could make sense of it herself. She shifted her hips, and Jay's fingers slipped, gliding into even more warmth. She hesitated for a moment, but Nicole stroked the side of her cheek in encouragement. "I love you. I want you inside me."

Her instincts screamed for her to push forward, to part the heated velvet at her fingertips. She looked into Nicole's eyes and found nothing but trust. Slowly, she pressed past Nicole's entrance and into tight, clinging silk. It only took one thrust. She sank as deep as possible, and her thumb settled in place over the tight bud of Nicole's clit. A sob broke in her throat, and she realized that she was crying. She tried to blink back her tears, but Nicole brushed them away. "You deserve this, Jay. You deserve me. One bad thought doesn't cancel out all the good you've brought into my life."

A thousand protests formed in her head, but they all stuck in her throat. As long as Nicole was willing to forgive her, she could forgive herself, too. She rested their foreheads together, enjoying the softness of Nicole's palm against her cheek. Her hand started moving, and she savored the ripples around her fingers every time she hooked them. She tried to draw the same circles she had used before, and soon Nicole was bucking against her hand and screaming into her lips.

She didn't expect it to happen so fast. One moment, Nicole was rocking beneath her. The next, she was shaking apart. She let out a sharp cry, and her muscles locked up. Jay felt them pull impossibly tight, then loosen in a series of rolling shudders. The firm bud beneath her thumb pulsed, and a rush of wetness spilled into her hand, dripping down past her wrist. She kept thrusting, catching against the swollen spot along Nicole's front wall until the flood eased and the waves faded to weak flutters.

It only took Nicole a few seconds to recover. Her face relaxed into a satisfied smile, and her breasts rose and fell as she panted. "God, you're beautiful," she whispered. "I've never seen so much love in someone's eyes."

Jay laughed. "You've never called me that before."

"Called you what?"

"Beautiful. You've called me handsome, sexy...a bunch of other adjectives. But never beautiful."

"Well, you are beautiful. Always. Inside and out. Even when you're an idiot. Especially when you're an idiot for me."

Jay leaned in for another kiss, losing herself in Nicole's lips. Soft hands urged her to flip over, and she rolled onto her back, waiting to see what her lover had in mind. She gasped and arched her back as Nicole's hot mouth blazed along her neck. Feeling the edges of Nicole's teeth made her heart race, but it didn't hurt. The slight vulnerability highlighted how safe she felt, and a low throb shot between her legs.

Nicole didn't stop at the base of her throat. She lingered there for a moment, sucking the sensitive patch of skin over Jay's pulse point, but soon continued downward. Jay wove her fingers through Nicole's hair, unsure whether to push her further, or hold her in place when she found a nice spot. Warmth sealed over the tip of her breast, and sharp nails raked up along her inner thigh.

"I...I love you," Jay said, clutching at the back of Nicole's head. Her voice shook, but she couldn't keep the words back. Now that she had unlocked them, she wanted to keep saying them forever.

Nicole released her nipple, blowing a cool stream of air over the tip. "You're gonna love me even more in about ten seconds."

She tried to respond, but her voice was lost as Nicole covered her stomach with kisses. They trailed down the middle of her torso, traveling back and forth between her hips. She spread her knees apart and allowed Nicole to settle between them, resting her weight on her elbows and staring in awe. Nicole just gave her a dimpled smile before slowly lowering her head.

The first scrape of Nicole's tongue made her hips jerk. Her eyes rolled back in her head, and the throbbing became a deep, pounding ache. Nicole latched onto her clit, and the heat was almost too much. She quivered, clutching the afghan with fumbling fingers. Nicole moaned around her, and the vibrations threatened to send her over the edge early.

Just when she thought she was lost, the warmth eased away. She stared in disbelief, whining as Nicole's lips moved outward to graze her inner thigh. "You didn't think I'd let you off that easy, did you?" she murmured.

Jay swallowed. She rolled her hips forward, but her goal remained out of reach. It wasn't until she held still and waited that Nicole finally took pity on her. The warmth returned, but it was softer and less focused, covering more of her at once. She shivered with each scrape of Nicole's tongue, but managed to keep still.

The next few minutes were a blur. Nicole dragged her up to the edge over and over again, painting circles with her tongue, sucking the point of her clit, and even sliding down to thrust past her entrance. It left her dizzy and breathless, and she couldn't stay upright. She fell flat on her back, staring at the ceiling as red crept in around her eyes. One of her hands shot out to clutch the back of Nicole's head, but it barely made a difference. The slow, torturous pace didn't speed up.

Jay couldn't tell how long Nicole spent teasing her. It stretched into an endless thread, with no beginning or end in sight. Every strand of muscle in her body pulled taut, and she bucked against Nicole's mouth, praying she wouldn't be denied again. "Please," she begged, fisting Nicole's hair with one hand and the afghan with the other. "Please, make me...I...I need to..."

Nicole brushed a wet, open kiss across the very tip of her clit.

"Need to what, baby?"

"Come," she blurted out, crying to the ceiling. "Fuck, I need to come."

Jay let out a sob of relief as Nicole's lips finally closed back around her. The pressure was enough to send her flying. Her mouth fell open, and she shouted something like Nicole's name as all the tension finally unraveled. The shaft of her clit twitched in Nicole's mouth, and a surge of heat spilled from deep inside her. It splashed across her thighs, running down along Nicole's chin, but the mess didn't matter. Something beautiful had slipped back into place, and she felt whole again.

Eventually, the fluttering pulses inside of her stilled. Nicole drew back, sighing and shaking her head as she examined the afghan. "Damn it, Jay. Now I have to throw this in the wash before bed." She pretended to sound annoyed, but her laughter made it clear that she was actually proud.

"Sorry," Jay mumbled. She didn't have enough strength left for more than one word. It took Nicole's help and a few failed attempts before she managed to sit up.

"Don't worry. I'll take care of it after I tuck you in."

She blinked in surprise. "You mean I get to stay the night?"

"Were you not there for the amazing sex we just had?" Nicole folded an arm around her shoulder to help keep her upright, sliding the afghan out from under their legs. "You could stay with me every night from now on, and I'd be thrilled. How else are we going to make love when we wake up tomorrow morning?"

Jay beamed. "Make love?"

Nicole gave her a soft look. "I choose my words for a reason. Now come on. I don't want you passing out on my floor."

Chapter Sixteen

JAY SAT UP WITH a start. Her eyes snapped open and a trail of cold sweat trickled down her back. She took in several quick breaths, unable to calm her racing heart. Her eyes darted around the unfamiliar room, trying to figure out what had woken her, but it was too dark to see. She almost jumped out of her skin as something warm and soft moved beside her. *Oh! Nicole. Still not used to that.*

"S'wrong?" Nicole slurred, squinting up at her. She tried to say something else, but a yawn broke through instead.

"I'm fine. I must have had a bad dream or something."

Nicole burrowed back under the covers, opening her arms in invitation. "Aww. C'mere and let me cuddle you. We should get back to..."

A soft noise from beyond the bedroom door made them both flinch. They looked at each other with wide eyes, and Nicole whispered in a trembling voice. "Oh God. Someone's in my house."

Jay swallowed, trying not to panic. "Do you have your phone?"

Nicole shook her head. "It's downstairs. We have to go get it."

"Are you crazy?" Jay hissed. Instead of being afraid, she was angry at Nicole's recklessness. *Shit. A crazy person totally* would *murder my girlfriend right after we made up.* "Don't you watch horror movies? We want to avoid the spooky, dangerous hallway. The person who investigates *always* dies first."

There were more muffled footsteps, but Nicole's face set with determination. "No. I need to see who it is. It has to be a member of my family..." Her voice trailed off, but she didn't have to say the rest. Whoever had broken into the house was probably the same person who had killed Mr. Fox. Before Jay could protest, Nicole climbed out of bed and threw on a nightshirt. "Come on. It's two against one if you come with me. I like those odds."

Jay scrambled for the pair of stolen boxers near the foot of the bed.

She couldn't let Nicole go out and face whoever it was alone. Once they were somewhat covered, they moved toward the door. On impulse, Jay unplugged the lamp and removed it from the nightstand, gripping it in her hands like a weapon. The metal slipped in her sweaty palms, and she had to clench hard to keep from dropping it. Hopefully, whoever was sneaking around the house wasn't carrying something worse.

They crept into the hallway as quietly as possible, shoulders pressing close together. The noises stopped, and they froze, certain their quarry had heard them. After several heartbeats of silence, a loud crash echoed through the house. Movement shifted near the banister, and someone started thumping down the stairs.

Nicole moved to follow, but Jay held out her hand. "Don't! If they're running away, we shouldn't run after them."

"But—"

"We can figure this out," Jay said, praying Nicole would listen. "Chasing a killer is a *really* bad idea."

Nicole frowned, but didn't run down the stairs after the shadow. Instead, she walked over to the last place they had seen it. "No sign of anyone. I guess we scared them off."

Jay's shoulders sank, and she heaved a grateful sigh of relief. "Good. What was that crashing sound?"

"I'm not sure. It might have come from my office. Wait, let me get the light." Nicole felt her way across the wall and flicked the nearest switch. It took several moments for Jay's eyes to adjust, but when they did, she realized what was wrong immediately. A shelf just inside Nicole's office had tipped over, and several books were scattered across the floor. "I knew I should have paid to build shelves directly into the walls," Nicole sighed. "But what the hell would a thief or a murderer want with my Romance Novels?"

Jay groaned at her girlfriend's completely underwhelmed reaction. *Of course she's not upset over the fact that we both could have been killed. We need to figure this out, and fast, before something worse happens.* "I don't have a clue, but I know someone else who might."

A grin spread across Nicole's face. "Really? You mean it?"

"Yup. Really. I can't believe I'm saying this, but we need to call Aunt Mimi."

***

"So, what made you change your mind?" Nicole asked. "Last time I checked, you didn't want your aunt snooping around anymore crime scenes."

Jay removed her cup from the coffee maker and set it down on the counter. "I realized I've been wrong about a lot of things," she said, a little sheepishly. "You most of all, but I could have treated Memma better, too. She's a lot smarter than I give her credit for, even if she is crazy."

"What does that mean, by the way? Memma? I've been meaning to ask."

"It means 'Aunt' in Malayalam. It's a term of endearment. Kind of like Auntie, I guess. She calls me 'muthey', which means pearl." She opened the cupboard above the coffee maker and frowned in disappointment. "Do you have any sugar around here? Cream too, if you've got it."

"I've got both. Sorry, they aren't near the coffee because I don't use them." Nicole gave her a wink, brushing by on her way to the pantry. "I take mine dark."

Jay rolled her eyes. "Ha, very funny. I've seen that movie, you know." She took the offered bowl of sugar and scooped a generous amount into her cup. Then, she opened the refrigerator in search of cream. "This feels weird, doesn't it? Making coffee like normal people an hour after someone broke in."

"What else do you want us to do? We checked the rest of the house, and your aunt Mimi's on her way. Wait, has it really been an hour?" Nicole's brow furrowed, and she checked the stove clock. "What's taking her so long?"

"Are you kidding? Aunt Mimi's always late. When we moved from London to Toronto, she showed up five minutes before the flight left with a dozen different purses. She had to check all of them before they let her on." The doorbell rang as soon as she finished. "Told you. Let's go get her."

Aunt Mimi greeted them with a smile when they opened the door. This time, she was carrying a white purse with purple flowers, and against all odds, she had managed to find matching footwear. Jay stifled a laugh. It looked more like a wallpaper pattern than a fashion statement. "Sorry I'm late. Tinkerbelle didn't want to come."

"Good thing," Jay muttered. She clutched her mug of coffee protectively to her chest.

"So, what's this about a break-in?"

"Here," Nicole said, "it's probably easier if we show you." Together, the three of them headed up the stairs and into the office. The pile of books and the broken shelf were still spread across the floor.

"Hmm." Aunt Mimi reached up to adjust her horn-rimmed glasses, peering closely at the mess. She bent down, examining a dog-eared copy of *San Diego Sunsets* with great interest. Nicole blushed, and Jay cleared her throat. "Are you sure this is the only part of the house the murderer was in?"

"Pretty sure." Jay leaned against the desk and set her coffee down beside the keyboard. "We actually interrupted them. They ran when they heard our footsteps."

Nicole took a seat in the office chair. "We did a sweep of the house before you got here. Nothing else was missing." Despite her earlier bravery, Jay could tell she was a little shaken. Her eyes were wider than usual, and her fingers trembled around her coffee cup. "I checked my files right after Jay called you, but nothing involving Grandpa's will or the Fox Foundation was taken. I have no idea what they wanted."

Aunt Mimi straightened and turned to look at Nicole. "Did you or Jay lock the door when you came in?"

Nicole shook her head and set her cup down without taking a sip. "No. I rarely do when I'm home. I never thought something like this would happen in my neighborhood...to me..." She gave a short, nervous laugh. "I guess that's pretty stupid, isn't it? I never thought anyone in my family would be murdered, either."

Jay reached out to hold her hand. "It's my fault," she said, stroking the side of Nicole's wrist with her thumb. "I was the one who came barging into your house at three in the morning."

"I'm glad you did." Nicole gave her a weak smile. "Otherwise, I would have been alone when...Okay, that train of thought isn't making me feel any better. Let's talk about something else."

"How about these books?" Aunt Mimi said. She walked over to the desk and stepped aside, giving Nicole a clear view of the haphazard pile. "Start putting them back up and tell me if anything is missing from the shelf."

Obediently, Nicole left the chair and knelt down to sort through the pile. She began putting the books back on the shelf, and Jay reached for her mug, blinking tiredness from her eyes. "Nothing so far," Nicole said as she slid a stack of paperbacks into place. "I don't seem to be missing anythi...Wait." She stood up, running her hands over the books that hadn't been knocked over. "My photo album. The big white one I keep on the middle shelf. It's not here."

"A photo album?" Jay made a sour face, grimacing as she swallowed a mouthful of unsweetened coffee. Apparently, she hadn't grabbed her own cup after all. "That's strange. What would a murderer want with that?" Realization dawned, and her eyes widened. "Oh shit," she murmured, setting the cup down in shock. All of the pieces fell into place, and she felt like the wind had been knocked out of her chest.

Nicole turned toward her. "'Oh shit,' you just drank my coffee? Seriously, did we not just have an entire conversation about how I take mine black?"

"No, it's—"

Aunt Mimi let out a loud shout. "That's it!" She threw up her arms in triumph, and Jay nearly dropped her cup of coffee. "I've solved it! I can't believe I didn't realize before. I was so blind."

"Wait, how did you solve it? You weren't even there when Tom and I—"

But Aunt Mimi continued talking over her. "We have to get everyone together. Make plans, invitations..."

Jay stood up. "First, let's make sure we're on the same page. It was a mistake—"

"Right! And then the killer panicked, so they hid the strychnine back in the shed *after*..."

"...and you weren't there, but Nicole mentioned the wedding the other day..."

"So the only thing to do was break into her house and take the album."

"Wait a minute." Nicole rested her hands on her hips, glaring at both of them. "You two aren't making sense. If you know who did it, tell me. In plain English, please."

Jay's momentary elation faded in an instant. Her heart sank, and she gave Nicole a sad look. Aunt Mimi gave her arm an encouraging squeeze. "You explain, muthey. I'm going to use Nicole's phone for a minute and make a few calls. We need to end this."

Jay nodded. "Fair enough. I think it's better to take care of this privately before we bring the police in. They'll probably think we're crazy anyway."

Aunt Mimi smiled. "Aren't we?" She left the study a moment later, leaving Jay alone with Nicole.

"All right, you'd better sit back down for this one. It's not what you think."

Chapter Seventeen

I DIDN'T THINK IT was possible for a Fox family gathering to be even more awkward than last time, Jay thought. She glanced around the room, eyes flitting from face to face. She had no idea how Aunt Mimi had persuaded everyone to return to Stephen Fox's mansion, but they were all gathered in the sitting room, some more reluctantly than others.

Aunt Martha looked irritated, and the corners of her mouth were pulled down in a frown. She was complaining to Bill, who kept mopping his forehead with his ever-present handkerchief. Denise remained relatively unaware of what was happening, chewing her gum as she scrolled through something on her phone.

Tom Junior was silent and sulky, as usual. He sat next to Patrick, although the two of them remained a good distance apart on the couch. Jay suspected the flask in Tom's coat pocket was filled with something strong. Their mother Beatrice was already well on her way to intoxication. Unlike the others, she had been brave enough to take a drink from the liquor cabinet, although she had prepared it herself.

Janine was seated on the other side of the fire. She looked even unhappier than Tom Junior, and her lips were pressed into a stiff line. Gregory Fox followed Denise's example, staring at his phone in a desperate attempt to ignore everyone else. Jay glanced away before they noticed her staring. That left Nicole on her right and Harry on her left. Both of them looked understandably nervous. Aunt Mimi was still nowhere to seen.

"Where is she?" Nicole whispered beside her ear.

"Dunno." Jay turned in her seat. Nicole's face looked pale, and with their arms pressed together, she could feel every tremble of her lover's body. She wanted to reach out and offer comfort, but Janine's glare made her nervous. Eventually, she decided it didn't matter. Gathering her courage, she slid her arm behind Nicole's shoulders and gave her a reassuring squeeze. "Hey, are you okay? There's still time to back out."

Nicole shook her head. "No. We…I…have to do this."

"She can't be long now." Jay shot a hopeful glance toward the door to the sitting room. "Think she's planning a dramatic entrance?"

"Probably."

Their guess was confirmed a few moments later. The doors to the sitting room flew open, and Aunt Mimi strode in with Tinkerbelle in her arms. The whole room turned as one, and there were a few confused murmurs. "Thank you all for coming," she said, passing through her seated audience to stand in front of the fire. "For those of you who don't know me, I'm Mimi Venkatesan, Jay's aunt."

Janine's eyes flashed, and she made as if to rise from her seat. "I'm only going to say this once," she snapped, articulating every word. "Leave, or I'll have to call the police." Her eyes zeroed in in Tinkerbelle, who growled in recognition. "And take that awful dog with you."

"Don't bother, Aunt Janine," Tom Junior said. A sick smile spread across his face as he glanced around the room. "This has been a long time in coming. Aren't you curious about what the amateur sleuth has to say?"

Janine sat back down in her chair. She didn't say a word.

"Well, I think the dog is cute," Denise said brightly. Tinkerbelle kept growling, but her tail wagged in approval.

"Wait, you're the one who invited us?" Bill asked. "I thought this was about the will. If it's not, I'm leaving." He tucked his handkerchief away and started to get up as well, but froze when Tinkerbelle peeled her lips back over her fangs.

"Not quite," Aunt Mimi said. He sat back down, and Tinkerbelle stopped snarling. "The message you got today didn't come from Mr. Matheson. It came from me."

So, that's how she got them here, Jay thought. Aunt Mimi was devious, even if she was more than a little delusional, too.

"Don't tell me you've actually figured it out," Harry said, looking at her admiringly. "Well? Tell us. Do the big reveal!"

"I have," Aunt Mimi said proudly, "with some help from your sister." Harry turned to look at Nicole, but she avoided his eyes. "Yes, Nicole helped too, but that wasn't the sister I meant."

"This is ridiculous," said Janine. "I'm not going to listen to you throw around anymore accusations. And bringing *her* into this..."

"Same here," Bill said. "This was a mistake."

"Nooo," Beatrice said, drawing out the word longer than necessary.

She clapped a heavy hand on Bill's shoulder. "C'mon, stay. I wanna hear what thish person hash to say."

"Tom Junior, Patrick," Aunt Martha shouted, glaring at them both. "Your mother is assaulting my husband." Tinkerbelle let out a nervous bark at the loud noise, and everyone glared at each other.

"Shut up, Martha," Tom said. "Bill's a weasel, and she's too drunk to know what she's doing."

Aunt Mimi cleared her throat, directing the room's attention back on her. Everyone went silent, even Tinkerbelle. "There. That's better. As I was saying, I've discovered several things about the Fox family over the past week." She turned to look at Janine. "Your first husband, Richard, died under sudden and mysterious circumstances, and you received a huge payoff from his life insurance. Isn't that true?"

Janine folded her arms over her chest and looked away. "You already know it is."

Next, Mimi turned to Uncle Bill. "And you, Mr. Rorsche, owe a huge debt to Carlo Ritornello thanks to your gambling habit."

Bill swallowed down the visible lump in his throat and refused to answer.

Last, Aunt Mimi focused her attention on Tom Junior. "And don't think I've forgotten about you. I know why you're clutching that flask so tight, and I can't say I blame you. I'd probably drown my fears in alcohol too, if someone had tried to poison me."

Everyone started talking at once.

"Oh my God..."

"Him, too?"

"She's lying!"

"But it doesn't make sense."

Tinkerbelle let out a loud bark, quieting the crowd. Aunt Mimi coughed and ignored the outburst. "The biggest clue came from the break-in at Nicole's house this morning." There were several murmurs of confusion. "Only one thing was taken: a family photo album. That's when I knew. The money, the motives, none of it mattered. And when Jay accidentally drank from Nicole's cup this morning, the final piece made sense. Stephen Fox was never the intended target. Tom Junior was."

Janine's angry expression faltered, changing to one of total shock. Bill dropped his handkerchief. Beatrice started wailing, and Patrick looked over at his brother in stunned silence. Even Martha was speechless.

At last, Tom Junior spoke up. His voice shook, and the haunted look on his face was a complete contrast from his usual smarmy expression. It reminded Jay of the brief flash of terror she had caught during their conversation in the parking lot. "But if it wasn't Nicky who tried to kill me...then who?"

"You weren't far off, Tom," Aunt Mimi said. She gave him an almost approving smile. "Someone did plant that strychnine in the garden shed after the murder to make you look guilty, the same someone who tried and failed to kill you with the dose he brought in his pocket. But he poisoned the wrong glass, and you suspected the wrong sibling."

They all turned to look at Harry. Several emotions crossed his face at once. Surprise, disbelief, pain, and grief. At last, he settled on anger. "You don't know what you're talking about," he said, clenching his fists at his sides.

"She does, Harry," Nicole murmured. She stood up from the couch and turned, staring down at him with glistening eyes. "Once Jay told me what happened, I knew it was the truth. We were the ones who found Tori's body." Her voice caught, and she took in a shuddering breath, blinking back tears. "She was wearing her wedding dress. That's why you had to steal the photo album. When I told you I had it at the lawyer's office, you thought I might look at it and remember. I should have realized sooner. Yellow was her favorite color."

Harry refused to look at Nicole's face. His entire body vibrated, as if he was about to spring from his chair. Jay tensed beside him, preparing to jump up as well. "You don't have any proof," he said, but the words were far from convincing.

"But we do," Aunt Mimi said. "That's why we found the yellow garter under Stephen Fox's body. Unfortunately, it turned out to be the wrong body. It was a garter from your sister's wedding outfit. I suspect you kept it with you as a keepsake, a reminder of your revenge. When you bent over to inspect the body, you impulsively decided to leave it there to let your cousin know that he hadn't gotten away with his actions, and he was going to pay for them. It was a stupid thing to do, but angry people aren't always logical. And you were still angry, weren't you, about Victoria's death?"

The sound of Victoria's name broke the tension. Harry launched out of his seat, shoving past Nicole and rushing for Tom Junior. "You *killed* her," he shouted, his face a mask of fury. "You killed my sister with your stupid joke."

"Get away from me!" Tom panicked and tried to run, but Harry was faster. He lunged, and they toppled onto the couch, knocking it over backward.

"Harry, don't!" Nicole screamed. She tried to pull them apart, but she tripped and Harry's elbow jabbed into her stomach. Spit flew from Tom's mouth as Harry squeezed down on his throat, but he couldn't wriggle free.

There wasn't time to be afraid, or even to think. Nicole needed her help. Jay leapt up from her seat and took Nicole's place, trying to break Harry's grip. Like a frightened, confused animal, Harry let go of Tom and whirled on her. Jay grabbed his shoulders, trying to hold him back, but he was much stronger than she was. Just as Patrick and Gregory Fox flew out of their seats to help, he pulled her over the couch with him. His fist connected with her gut, and her stomach screamed. She flinched and tried to curl up, certain the next blow would make her pass out. *Fuck, fuck, fuck, what have I gotten myself into?*

Before Harry could get in another punch, a loud, yapping bark sounded next to her ear. She opened her eyes in time to see Tinkerbelle leap over the toppled couch, teeth bared and fur bristling. The tiny poodle launched at Harry, landing between his knees and latching on to his left leg.

"What the—get it off!" He tried to kick Tinkerbelle, and Jay reacted on instinct. She threw her fist out, and somehow, it connected with flesh. Harry staggered away from her, bringing his hands up to his face as blood spurted from between his fingers. He tried to move, but Tinkerbelle's hold on his pants tripped him up. He fell flat onto the ground, flailing as Tinkerbelle tore through the bottom of his trousers.

When Jay looked up, everyone else was out of their chairs, shouting and waving their arms. Most of them were no help at all. "Nicole! Call Lieutenant Slack," Aunt Mimi shouted as Harry tried to make another lunge for freedom, or for Tom. Thankfully, Patrick forced him to the ground as Aunt Mimi scooped up the snarling Tinkerbelle.

Nicole hurried to pull out her phone. "Lieutenant Slack...? Yes...yes, this is Nicole Fox. My brother's attacking...no...no...I can't explain...It's violent, isn't that enough? Just get here! The Fox mansion. Hurry!"

The rest of the short, tense conversation was lost on Jay. Her heart was pounding too loud for her to hear anything else, but she saw when Harry stopped struggling in Patrick's grip. He went limp, hanging his head and burying his face in his bloody hands. His body trembled, and he began to weep.

Chapter Eighteen

"YOU REALIZE WHAT A mess this is, don't you?" Slack asked. He began counting on his fingers and his voice grew louder with each word. "Assault, obstruction of justice, disturbing the peace, interfering in a police investigation...I can think of at least ten other things to charge you with."

"I know, sir," Jay said, trying her best to sound repentant. She had to play to Slack's sympathies. The last thing Nicole needed was to see her get thrown in lock-up along with Harry. "I'm sorry we didn't call you sooner, but I thought Nicole deserved an explanation. After everything she's been through, Harry owed her that much."

Slack's jowls quivered. His thick lips were still pulled in a frown, but she thought she saw a hint of sympathy in his eyes. "You were lucky, Miss Venc...Jay. He could have seriously harmed someone if you hadn't clocked him." For just a moment, a hint of a smile broke through his businesslike expression. "It was a good hit. Although I hear you had a little back-up."

Jay shrugged, averting her eyes. Her fist was still tingling, and her stomach ached. Even though Harry had started it, she felt bad for punching him. The only good thing about the situation was that Nicole hadn't seemed mad at her, and she hadn't panicked yet despite having a hundred good reasons. Deep down, she was almost a little proud of herself.

"So, are there any other secrets you've been hiding besides the identity of the murderer?" Slack asked. "Now's the time. I want a full disclosure."

She thought for a moment. "Well, Harry also broke into Nicole's house early this morning. Nicole had Victoria's old family album in her office, and he was afraid she'd look at it and remember the wedding colors. Once we realized what he'd taken, we figured out the real motive, and everything else fell into place. "

Slack took the seat across from her and rested his elbows on the table. "If Harry was afraid Nicole would recognize the garter, why did he leave it at the crime scene? Most people would have backed off once they realized they poisoned the wrong guy instead of throwing clues on the ground."

"Aunt Mimi had a theory about that. This murder was supposed to be justice for Victoria. Harry probably brought it with him as a reminder. But when he killed his grandfather by accident, he wanted Tom Junior to know the poison was meant for him. So he left the garter as a threat when he bent down to move the body." She shuddered as she remembered the haunted look on Tom Junior's face. "I actually think it worked. Tom Junior seemed squirrely every time I talked to him. But then Nicole mentioned the photo album, and Harry got scared. He knew he had to take it before she put the pieces together, too."

Slack ran a hand through his thinning hair and shook his head. "It all sounds crazy, but I think you're right. Everything fits. There are still a few pieces missing, but..." He heaved a sigh. "Anything else?"

"Not that I can think of."

"Then you're free to go." Slack heaved himself back out of the chair and opened the door for her.

Jay sucked her lower lip between her teeth. "How long do you think Harry will be in prison?"

Slack gave a noncommittal grunt. "No way to say. The jury could go easy. You know, since it was for his dead sister. If he ends up with a really good lawyer, they might put him in a psych ward for a while. Either way, I hope they make him visit a shrink. He needs it."

She nodded in agreement. Despite his ability to plot out the murder, something was definitely wrong with Harry. With a sigh, she let go of her pity for him and re-focused on Nicole. She was the one who had suffered the most in all this.

Slack seemed to read her mind. "Go spend some time with your girlfriend. She's going to need a shoulder." He paused, and his small smile returned. "And tell that aunt of yours to stay the hell away from mystery solving for a while. She already stole our collar. We don't want her stealing our jobs, too."

***

Jay glanced nervously from side to side, finally letting her eyes settle on her shoes. Her brief interview with Lieutenant Slack had ended a while ago, but she was still waiting for Nicole to finish her turn. Unfortunately, she was not waiting alone. Janine Fox sat next to her in the front room of the police station, trying to avoid the eyes of the curious receptionist. Her face was paler than usual and her shoulders slumped with exhaustion.

Finally, Jay couldn't stand another second of silence. "I owe you an apology," she blurted out, twisting her hands in her lap and fixing her gaze anywhere but on Janine's face.

Janine looked up in surprise. "For what?" Her voice sounded tired, Jay realized. It made sense, after everything that had happened that evening.

"I'm sorry we followed you to your hair appointment," she admitted, more than a little embarrassed. "While I'm at it, I might as well apologize for the time Aunt Mimi trashed our dinner. I tried to talk her out of it."

Janine sighed, and Jay looked up. "If tonight's taught me anything, it's that we can't control anyone else's actions. There are worse things your aunt could have done."

"I know, but I figured I should apologize anyway," Jay mumbled. "What she did wasn't right. I should have tried harder to stop her."

"I don't hold you responsible, but thank you for the apology." To her surprise, Janine gave her a soft smile. "She's really clever, your aunt Mimi. Definitely crazy, but clever. I'm amazed she figured it out. Without her..." Her voice trailed off, and Jay's stomach lurched. *Without her, Harry wouldn't have been arrested.*

"I'm sorry..."

"Don't be. Stephen was a good man. Maybe this will bring him some peace, especially if Harry gets the help he needs."

"He was a good man. I'm sorry I only got to meet him once." She took a deep breath in through her nose. "I'm really serious about my relationship with Nicole." Despite her strong feelings, it was a difficult confession to put into words, especially to someone else. "I want to start off on the right foot this time with you and the rest of the family. I don't want anything Aunt Mimi did to change things."

Janine locked eyes with her, and she struggled not to squirm in her seat. "Nicole is an adult, and I'm not her biological mother. Why are you trying so hard?"

"Because I love her," she said softly. "She deserves a family that gets along."

Janine shook her head. "I think it's a little late for that. The Fox family was dysfunctional long before you came in to the picture."

"I guess you don't choose the family you marry in to," Jay said, mostly to herself. "Well, I mean, you do, but—"

"You don't choose who you fall in love with."

"Yeah. That's what I meant."

"Would you believe that I married Nicole's father because of his personality and not his money?" Janine smiled, obviously revisiting a pleasant memory. "We knew each other while my first husband was still alive. He was a good friend."

Jay got the sense that Janine was sharing something very personal with her, and she was strangely touched. "I never thought I'd end up in a long-term relationship," she said, deciding to share something personal about herself in return. "I was always too quiet. Too nervous about what other people thought of me. Then Nicole came along. I know she talks a mile a minute, but she hears me, too. She's the first person who gave a shit about what I had to say. I was whipped before I knew it."

"What's that about you being whipped?" She and Janine looked up with one movement when they heard Nicole's familiar voice.

Jay stood up and opened her arms. When Janine gave her an encouraging nod, she gave Nicole a short, sweet kiss on the lips. "Oh, I was just telling your stepmother how you're the boss in our relationship."

"You got that right," Nicole said. Jay could tell she was trying to sound cheerful, but her slouched posture and the dark circles under her eyes gave her away. She looked exhausted. "Hey, Mom. Where's Dad?"

Jay stepped back, and Janine stepped in for a hug as well. "He went across the street to get some coffee. I have the feeling we're all going to be drinking a lot of caffeine in the near future."

"Why are you waiting here for me?"

"Would you believe I wanted to see if you were all right?"

"No, I'm not," Nicole said. "I just can't believe Harry would hurt anyone, even Tom Junior."

"I don't think he's really Harry right now," Jay said. A hurt look crossed Nicole's face, and she hurried to explain herself. "Something must have changed in him when Victoria killed herself. I think he needs psychological help."

"And a good lawyer," Nicole added bitterly.

She reached out to take Nicole's hand, running her thumb over the back of her knuckles. "What I mean is, he isn't the same brother you grew up with. Don't let what happened now take that away."

Nicole sighed. "How did you get to be so smart growing up as an only child?"

"I'm related to my aunt Mimi. Of course I'm smart."

"And a little crazy," Nicole added.

Even Janine had to smile at that. "So, where do we go from here? As a family."

"I don't know what to do about Harry. Rehab would be a good idea for Tom Junior, but he won't listen."

"You might be surprised," Jay said. "He looked pretty affected by what happened tonight."

"I'll talk to his parents," Janine offered. "I agree that rehab is probably the best place for him. Actually, Thomas Sr. and Beatrice could both stand to drink a little less alcohol and spend a little more time with their sons."

"What about Uncle Bill?"

Janine frowned. "Let him get out of that one on his own. He and Martha aren't exactly in the poor house."

"And Harry?" Nicole asked in a soft voice.

Janine reached out to squeeze her shoulder. "We'll do what we can for him. He fooled all of us. Only Jay's aunt Mimi had any idea. I'm still not sure how she put all the pieces together."

"Too much time on her hands and too many detective novels," Jay said. She gave Nicole and Janine a hesitant smile. Maybe things would get better now that Aunt Mimi had brought the truth out into the open. She hoped so.

"Come on." Nicole took her hand and smiled at Janine. "Let's go across the street and see if Dad got anything for us along with his coffee."

***

"I can't believe it's over," Nicole said as they pulled out of the coffee shop parking lot. Jay turned to look at her, but she was gazing out the passenger's side, watching the streetlights go by. All she could see was a glimpse of Nicole's white reflection in the window. "Is it wrong to feel relieved? Despite what Harry did, I'm glad we found out the truth."

Jay tapped the brake at a stoplight, drumming her fingers lightly on the steering wheel. "It's not wrong," she said at last. "I'm relieved, too. But I'm also worried."

"About Harry?"

"No. About you." The light turned green, and Jay pulled ahead into the darkness. "To be honest, I'm totally out of my depth here."

Slowly, Nicole turned her head. Her face was even paler than it had looked in the window. "You don't mean...you're not leaving me, right?"

Jay's eyes widened. "No! Of course I'm not leaving you. Hold on." She flipped her turn signal and pulled over to the side of the road, not paying attention to honking of the car behind her. She put the car in park and turned in her seat. "What makes you think I want to break up with you?"

Nicole sighed, slumping further in her seat. "Sorry. You didn't have to pull over. It just sounded like the beginning of a break-up speech. And with everything that's happened..." She looked up, and Jay gasped when she saw tears shining in Nicole's eyes. "My brother killed my grandfather, and I know for a while, you thought it might have been me. I wouldn't blame you for deciding to leave."

"Never." Jay unbuckled her seatbelt and leaned over, squeezing Nicole's hand tight in hers. "I just don't know how to comfort you. You've been through so much in a short amount of time."

"Yeah, but I wouldn't change it."

Her eyebrows lifted in surprise. "You wouldn't?"

Nicole gave her a small smile. "No. I wish my grandfather was alive again, and I wish my brother wasn't in jail. I wish my sister hadn't killed herself and my cousin wasn't an alcoholic. But I don't regret falling in love with you during all that. Not even a little."

"I feel helpless," she murmured, running her thumb along the curve of Nicole's wrist. "I don't know how to comfort you."

"Jay, you're anything but helpless. Besides, don't you remember what you did tonight? You leapt up to protect me without even thinking about it!" Nicole's fingers ghosted over her stomach, testing the sore muscles there. "You were so brave."

"I was only brave because I wasn't thinking about it," Jay mumbled, flushing with embarrassment. "Getting in a fistfight with your brother probably didn't help. I want to make you feel better, but I don't know how."

Her heart throbbed in her throat as Nicole's arms came up to wrap around her neck. "Oh, Jay. Just love me..." Before she could speak, Nicole's lips caught hers. Her eyes closed. Her heart throbbed. Her fingers wove through Nicole's hair, holding her close until she couldn't remember anything except the warmth, the softness, the sweetness of her mouth.

They kissed until her lungs burned for breath and she could barely remember her own name. Her name...Suddenly, she realized that Nicole didn't even know her full name. She pulled back, panting slightly. "Jayshree. My name is Jayshree."

"Jayshree," Nicole whispered, testing the name. A slow grin spread across Jay's face. She had never really liked her name, but she loved hearing it in Nicole's voice. "What does it mean?"

Jay blushed. "Goddess of Victory. I know it's a bit weird..."

Nicole laughed and leaned up for another kiss. This one was soft, but it still made every inch of her skin flush with heat. "It's beautiful. Just like you."

Epilogue: One Year Later

"I STILL CAN'T BELIEVE we have a dog," Jay said as she rested her head on Nicole's lap. She stared in disbelief at the tiny white ball of fuzz toddling around the living room, unable to keep from smiling. Watching the new puppy waddle across the carpet should have gotten boring over the past few weeks, but it was still adorable. It took an effort of will to keep from bombarding her friends and family with video clips. "If someone had told me a year ago that I would own a puppy, especially Tinkerbelle's evil spawn, I would have called them crazy."

Nicole started stroking her hair. "It's because you're a huge pushover. I thought I'd have to talk to you into it, or maybe even bribe you with sexual favors, but you fell in love with Wendy at first sight."

The puppy barked, her little pink tongue lolling from the corner of her mouth. "Hush, you," Jay threatened, "or I'll trade you in for a pit bull." Wendy fell over onto her back and stuck her paws straight up in the air, wiggling her hindquarters back and forth.

"Aw, you don't think Wendy is butch enough for you, handsome?" Nicole laughed. "Pit bulls really are the sweetest dogs, though. I had one growing up..."

Jay's breathing grew heavier as Nicole's soft fingers crept up along her arm. The touch was clearly meant to be seductive, and it sent a rush of warmth to some very pleasant places. "Don't start what you aren't willing to finish," she said, running her palm up along Nicole's thigh. The higher she climbed, the more heat she felt through the denim material of Nicole's jeans.

Nicole's hand covered hers, but not to stop its progress. Instead, she guided it higher. "Who said I wasn't willing to finish?"

"Really? We're going to do this in front of Wendy?"

"Of course not," Nicole drawled. "What kind of parent do you think I am? Wendy, close your eyes. Your mommies need some adult time."

Wendy took the sound of her name as an invitation. She scratched at the bottom of the sofa, begging to be picked up. Unable to resist the cuteness, Jay bent down and lifted her onto the couch. "I still hate your real mom, you know. Tinkerbelle didn't want to let me anywhere near you when we picked you out."

"There was no 'we' about it. You picked her out. I just sat and watched you hold her for the first hour because you didn't want to give her up."

Jay pouted. "I was training her to like me while she was still young and impressionable. Otherwise, her mom might have taught her to bite me or pee on me."

"Wendy does pee on you."

"But she's just a puppy. All puppies have accidents. Right, sweetie?" Wendy's answer was to yawn and curl up on Jay's stomach. "Don't get too comfortable there. I'm going to move in a minute once Nicole stops playing hard to get."

"I'm not playing hard to get. I was just about to get started before *someone* decided to turn this into a ménage á trois." The television grabbed Nicole's attention, and she reached for the remote, muting the sound. "Ugh, the last thing I want to hear about right now is that stupid trial. It's bad enough that most of us are being subpoenaed."

Jay's smile disappeared. "I still think it's shitty of them to drag you into court."

"Honestly, I'm not sure what I want the result of the trial to be. I hate what he did, and I miss Grandpa, but...he's my brother, you know? It hurts."

Jay rested her hand above Nicole's knee. "Making you testify against Harry isn't right. They have enough evidence to do it without you."

"I'm not testifying for or against him," Nicole said, but her voice wavered. They both knew her testimony would do more to hurt Harry than help him. "I wish I could just stay out of it."

"Well, your only way out is incestuous marriage," Jay said, trying to lighten the mood. "And I'd have a few objections to that."

"Ew. If you were hoping for sex after that comment, you might have just ruined your chances." There was a heavy pause, and Jay looked up in time to catch a curious expression on Nicole's face. "You've been mentioning marriage a lot lately. And with the dog and all...is there something you want to tell me?"

Heat rose in Jay's cheeks. She sat up, shifting Wendy onto her lap and clearing her throat. "Hey, I'll propose to you when I'm good and ready. Right, Wendy?" But Wendy was already asleep, and could not come to her defense. "Besides, you should take some time to think about it. Marrying me means you'll have to meet the rest of my crazy family, endure some really sexist wedding traditions, and eat a lot of spicy food."

Nicole's smile returned, and she leaned forward, resting their foreheads together and cupping the side of her face. "That's fine with me. I like Indian food."

Jay snorted, biting her lip to stifle her laughter. "Did you really just use that as a come-on?"

"Yup. I really did. Just don't wait too long, or I'll be too old to have your babies."

Her eyes popped open. "Babies?" she squeaked. "Um, honey..."

It was Nicole's turn to burst out laughing. Soon, Jay gave in and laughed along with her. The loud noise woke Wendy from her nap, and she whimpered her displeasure. Upset that her beauty sleep had been interrupted, she climbed down from the couch and wandered into the kitchen.

"So..." Nicole said, still gasping for breath. "I know we aren't ready for any real babies yet, but do you wanna practice anyway?"

"With lines like that, how can I resist?"

"Then let's move this to the bedroom. I have plans."

Jay grinned. Nicole's plans always turned out to be enjoyable. She wiggled free and hopped up from the couch, tapping the tip of Nicole's nose. "Tag. You're it." She sprinted for the bedroom as soon as Nicole lunged for her, laughing the whole way.

Her longer legs carried her to the bedroom first, but warm arms looped around her waist when she stopped to open the door. "You're an ass," Nicole said, searching for her zipper.

Jay shivered as the button of her jeans came undone. "*Your* ass."

"Not today. I'm still sore from last night."

"That's not what I..." Nicole nudged her forward into the bedroom, somehow managing to turn her around and start stripping off her clothes at the same time. "Meant?" Jay tried to help, but her hands only ended up getting in the way. Despite the playfulness of Nicole's actions, it was clear that she had a goal in mind. "What are you up to?" she asked, raising her arms so Nicole could yank her shirt over her head.

"I told you." Nicole scattered a few kisses across her shoulders, pausing to nip a sensitive spot behind her ear. The shirt fell to the floor at their feet. "I have plans." Her pants came next, shoved down into a wrinkled heap. Nicole gave her ass one last grope, sending her in the direction of the bedside drawer with a gentle slap. "Go strap up and get on the bed."

Jay's eyes widened in surprise, but the suggestion appealed to her immediately. Nicole always seemed to know what she wanted before she figured it out for herself. She sat on the edge of the bed and opened the nightstand. She found what she was looking for right on top—the double-sided cock Nicole had surprised her with a few months back. Its realism had thrown her a little at first, but it had quickly become her favorite. The fact that the smaller end fit inside her and the ridged seat rubbed over her clit were both bonuses.

"Well? Don't just stare at it." Jay glanced over her shoulder, and her jaw dropped. Nicole had already stripped naked. Her arms were stretched above her head as she pulled her hair into a messy knot, and the pose highlighted the curve of her breasts. "Great. Now you're staring at me."

"I can't help it. You're *naked*, and you're pulling your hair back, which means... things..."

Nicole gave her an expectant look, and Jay bent back over the drawer to find the lube. She poured some into her hand and smeared it over the shorter end of the toy, hoping her skin would warm it up. She tried not to tense her muscles as she worked the smaller half inside. This part was always awkward, especially with Nicole staring at her, but she had grown more comfortable with it as their relationship progressed. She knew Nicole wouldn't care if she looked a little silly.

Once the cock was securely in place, she hitched her boxers back up, leaving an impressive bulge at the front. "Better," Nicole said, swaying over to the bed and sliding onto the mattress.

Jay shivered as the edges of Nicole's nails raked along her stomach. They headed straight between her legs, easing the shaft out through the gap at the front of her boxers. "You're going to ruin these, aren't you?" she sighed, thighs flexing as Nicole's fist pulled up. The motion put pressure right against her clit, and she bit her lip, wondering if she had really needed the lube at all. *It's not fair how she can make me feel so good with one touch.*

"No. You are." Nicole's face hovered closer, and Jay groaned as their mouths finally met.

Somehow, Nicole's kisses still had the power to steal her breath. They made her body melt on first contact. She wound her arms around the back of Nicole's neck and parted her lips, but the slow burn didn't last long. Sleek legs hooked through hers, and all of a sudden, she was staring down into Nicole's eyes. While she tried to make sense of her flipped position, Nicole pushed up to nip the point of her chin. "What? I can't be on the bottom for once?"

Jay snorted. Even when Nicole was technically on the bottom, her bossiness never completely disappeared. Before she could say so, Nicole's hips rocked up against hers, and she let out a startled cry of pleasure. Without even trying, Nicole had found the perfect angle to grind against her. "You're mean," Jay gasped as Nicole began sliding along the underside of her shaft. The movement was slick, but the motion travelled all the way down to her clit.

"Not mean," Nicole purred, shifting so the head lined up with her entrance. Jay felt it start to slide forward, and her breath caught. The motion sent pressure straight back to the seat of the cock, pushing harder into her clit. "I promise I can be very, very nice."

The temptation was too much. Jay eased her hips forward, groaning into Nicole's mouth as she pushed inside. The tightness made her stomach tense, but it didn't stop her momentum. She wrapped her hands around Nicole's waist, but the grip wasn't enough to ground her. Her head spun, and the pace she had been trying to pick up stuttered before it even began.

"Don't be a tease," Nicole sighed, lips skimming over the planes of her face. "Take me. I want you to fuck me until I see stars."

Jay smiled. She could never deny Nicole anything. Pushing down her own desire to regain some control, she dragged one of Nicole's sleek legs around her waist and sank as deep as she could. Nicole hissed at the stretch, clawing between her shoulder blades. The hard red lines made Jay shudder, but the slight pain bled over into pleasure. Nicole always knew just how to encourage her.

Their lips met in another wet, open kiss as they found a shared rhythm. Jay buried her face in the sweet curve of Nicole's neck, nipping the soft skin there. Pressure swelled between her legs, but she ignored the way her clit throbbed against the ridged seat of the toy. She wanted to make Nicole come first. To feel those silky muscles clench around her and hear the greedy noises that spilled from Nicole's throat as she tipped over the edge.

"Oh God, more." The heat of Nicole's tongue trailed along her collarbone, and Jay's movements faltered. She shivered as Nicole's eager mouth latched to the base of her throat, sucking greedily at her pulse-point. She only broke away long enough to hiss, "Jay, harder..."

Hearing Nicole's usual demands melt into a plea almost made Jay melt as well. She sped up, tilting her chin to the side so Nicole could keep kissing the column of her throat. Each pump of her hips met the sweetest resistance, and every push coaxed out the most beautiful sounds. Beautiful, just like Nicole. Her heart ached as she looked into Nicole's dark, shining eyes. The desire there was all for her, and she drank it in.

But there was a teasing glint there as well, a spark of defiance that begged to be confronted. Jay slowed her thrusts, waiting until Nicole whimpered to speak. "Jay, what?" she asked, grinning as Nicole's nails hooked into her back. The slight pain sent a bolt of pleasure straight to her core, but she did her best to ignore it. It wasn't often she got her dominant girlfriend worked up enough to beg, and she didn't want to waste her chance.

"Christ, really?" Nicole glared up at her, but even her 'serious' expression was playful. Jay kept smiling at her in silence. "Oh, fine. Jay, *please.*"

Even though she knew she would pay dearly for it later, there was something satisfying about making Nicole plead. It made her feel confident in a way she couldn't describe, a way she hadn't even known was possible before they had fallen in love. Since she was already pushing her luck, she gave Nicole what she wanted. She angled her pelvis, making sure the tip of her cock hooked against Nicole's front wall on every backstroke.

The trick worked. Nicole stiffened and tried to shove a hand between their bodies, searching for her clit. Jay batted her hand away, taking over the job herself. She pinched the swollen bud between her fingertips, rocking it in and out of its hood. The scream she earned made her inner muscles clench around the shorter end of the shaft, and she knew she had to work fast. The new angle was better for her as well, and each thrust had her inner walls pulsing on the edge of a heavy climax of her own.

Thankfully, Nicole started to tremble before she got carried away. "Fuck, Jay, I'm gonna..." She never got to finish her sentence. She locked up and threw her head back against the pillow, bucking wildly as she shouted to the ceiling.

The harsh ripples of Nicole's inner walls tugged along Jay's length, and the rush of heat that followed made her lose focus. Her eyes glazed over, and she pumped forward one last time as bursts of warmth spilled between them. Feeling Nicole come was enough to release the pounding pressure inside her. She latched onto Nicole's shoulder, biting down as she released in deep, shuddering ripples. Her clit throbbed against the seat of the cock as Nicole's muscles squeezed down around her, and her hips jerked as she tried desperately to thrust deeper. Both of them arched in ecstasy, falling into a shared give and take.

Finally, the waves of bliss ended. Jay beamed down at Nicole, panting as she floated back to earth. Her efforts had left her exhausted and covered in a light sheen of sweat, but extremely satisfied. "Wow. That was *amazing*. You feel so good when you come around me..."

Nicole didn't respond. Her lashes fluttered, and her mouth spread in a devious smirk.

"Wh...what are you doing?" Jay asked, but Nicole cut off her words with a long string of kisses. She suddenly found herself flipped onto her back, and when she looked past her stomach, she was amazed to see that they were still joined. Her shaft was buried deep inside of Nicole, splitting her full outer lips into a pretty heart. "Fuck, how do you do that?"

Nicole laughed. "You knew that please was going to cost you," she teased, dragging her hips in a slow, circular motion. Even though it was subtle, it made stars explode behind Jay's eyes. There was even more sensation in this position, and she clutched at the sheets, trying to anchor herself. "But you like it best when I'm mean to you. I think that's why you made me say it."

Jay's breath hitched. Even though she had come once already, the fullness in her clit seemed to pulse all the way up along her length. She twitched with each press of Nicole's pelvis. "I...I was just..."

"Asking for it. You're lucky I want to come again. Otherwise, I'd torture you for a lot longer."

And there was really no other word to describe it. Nicole's manipulation of her body was nothing short of masterful. Jay keened as Nicole picked up a steady, slow grind, forcing the seat of the shaft up against her one moment and pulling back the next. The smaller end of the cock pushed into her front wall, making her ache with fullness. It was horrible and wonderful all mixed up, and she gave Nicole her most imploring look even though she knew it wouldn't work.

"Those sad eyes aren't going to get you what you want," Nicole murmured between quick kisses. "I'm not a pushover like you. Now, be good and ask nicely."

Jay chewed on her lower lip, unable to find the words. She clenched hard as Nicole started sliding up and down, and trails of warmth dripped along her thighs. At this angle, she could feel each shiver of Nicole's muscles as they squeezed around her cock. Her clit jumped with each shudder that travelled along its length, but even if she hadn't been able to feel anything, the sight of her shaft disappearing inside of Nicole again and again would have been enough to drive her crazy. The sight was entrancing, and she couldn't look away.

"Well? Do you have anything to say to me?" Nicole's fingertips dipped down, pulling her pouting lips apart to offer an even better view. A sob caught in Jay's throat before she could swallow it. The tip of Nicole's clit was blushing red, swollen and shimmering with wetness, and her entrance was stretched wide around the base of the tan shaft. It made her ache to thrust up even though she knew she'd be punished for it.

"Nicky, you're gorgeous," she blurted out, hoping it would be enough.

"That's nice," Nicole purred. She began playing with her clit, pushing back its hood and milking it between two fingers.

Jay watched in awe for several moments before she remembered the word she needed. "Please," she gasped, adding as much sincerity to her cracking voice as she could. "Please let me come."

"Fine. But only because you asked so nicely."

Nicole waited a beat to prove her point, then started riding in earnest, rolling her hips hard and fast. Jay could only handle the new speed for a few seconds. Something in her broke, and her hands shot out, seizing Nicole's waist. She brought their bodies together one last time, driving up as she spilled over. Her clit throbbed with each breaking wave, and her inner muscles clenched as she gave Nicole everything she had. Coming inside Nicole was the sweetest thing in the world, and her poor, strained body couldn't even hold everything she was feeling.

Somewhere between contractions, her lips stumbled over an 'I love you'. Even though her voice never joined the words, Nicole saw and smiled. To Jay's relief, it was enough to carry her lover over the edge with her. She felt Nicole's orgasm the second it hit. Everything tightened around her, then released as more warmth poured out around her shaft and splashed across her stomach. She caught a glimpse of Nicole's clit trapped between the edges of her frozen fingers, and she moved them aside again, taking over herself. More wetness slipped into her palm, but it only made her stroke the twitching bud faster. She wanted as much as she could coax free.

At last, both of them collapsed into a knot of arms and legs, so tangled together they couldn't possibly find their way free. Not that they wanted to. Jay heaved a contented sigh and slung her arms around Nicole's torso, pulling her close and kissing every inch of flesh she could reach. "I love you," she said, properly this time.

Nicole nipped at the edge of her ear, trapping her when she squealed and tried to wriggle away. "I love you, too."

Unfortunately, the tender moment was broken by an unwelcome buzzing sound. "Oh, come on," Jay groaned. "Who would call on my day off?" She slammed her hand across the nightstand, trying to find the source of the noise. At last, her fingers wrapped around her phone. She tilted the screen toward her face and closed her eyes, willing the name away.

"Who is it?" Nicole asked.

Jay turned the phone around to show her.

"You'd better answer it. She'll just keep calling until you do."

"I know," Jay said, pouting as Nicole dismounted and the wonderful weight lifted from her hips. "Hello, Memma. What is it?"

"Were you and Nicole having sex again? You sound out of breath..."

Jay rolled her eyes. "I thought we talked about this? There is *no* appropriate circumstance where you can ask that question."

"I suppose that's a yes. Well, I need you both to get dressed and head over to my house."

"Why?"

"Why else? We have another mystery on our hands. You didn't think I was going to retire after my first case, did you?"

"Well, I hoped..." Jay swung her legs over the edge of the bed, tucking the phone against her shoulder as she went in search of her shirt.

"Hoped for what?" Nicole asked, still staring at her with hooded eyes.

Jay sighed. Round two would have to wait for later. Unless...She covered the speaker with her hand. "I'll tell you in a second."

"Jay? Are you still there?"

"Yes, Aunt Mimi. I'm on my way. We'll be there in half an hour."

Nicole smiled, leaning back on her hands and folding her legs. It wasn't a particularly seductive pose, but somehow, she still managed to make it look like an invitation. "Half an hour? It only takes fifteen minutes to get to your aunt's house."

"I know," Jay said, offering Nicole her arm. "I thought we could use a shower first. Together. Naked."

Nicole took her arm, but used it to pull her into a standing embrace. "Jay Venkatesan, that sounds like an excellent idea."

The End

About Rae D. Magdon

Rae D. Magdon is a writer living and working in the state of Alaska. She has coauthored three books with Michelle Magly, *All the Pretty Things*, *Dark Horizons*, and *Starless Nights (Dark Horizons Book 2)*.

The first book in the Amendyr series *The Second Sister*, was published in March 2014 and was soon followed with *Wolf's Eyes*, published in August 2014. The third book of the series, *The Witch's Daughter* was released in April 2015. *Wolf's Eyes* and *Dark Horizons* were finalists in the 2014 Rainbow Awards SciFi/Fantasy category. *The Witch's Daughter* received an Honorable Mention and the cover was a finalist in Illustrations in the 2015 Rainbow Awards.

She enjoys writing fantasy and science fiction, in addition to modern-day romances. When she is not writing original fiction, she ~~wastes~~ spends her time dabbling in ~~unapologetically smutty~~ romantic lesbian fanfiction. In her free moments, which are few and far between, she enjoys spending time with Tory, her wonderful spouse, and their two cats.

Connect with Rae online

Website - http://raedmagdon.com/
Facebook - https://www.facebook.com/RaeDMagdon
Tumblr - http://raedmagdon.tumblr.com/
Email - rdmagdon@desertpalmpress.com

Other Books by Rae D. Magdon

Amendyr Series

The Second Sister
ISBN: 9781311262042
ELEANOR OF SANDLEFORD'S entire world is shaken when her father marries the mysterious, reclusive Lady Kingsclere to gain her noble title. Ripped away from the only home she has ever known, Ellie is forced to live at Baxstresse Manor with her two new stepsisters, Luciana and Belladonna. Luciana is sadistic, but Belladonna is the woman who truly haunts her. When her father dies and her new stepmother goes suddenly mad, Ellie is cheated out of her inheritance and forced to become a servant. With the help of a shy maid, a friendly cook, a talking cat, and her mysterious second stepsister, Ellie must stop Luciana from using an ancient sorcerer's chain to bewitch the handsome Prince Brendan and take over the entire kingdom of Seria.

Wolf's Eyes
ISBN: 9781311755872
CATHELIN RAYBROOK has always been different. She Knows things without being told and Sees things before they happen. When her visions urge her to leave her friends in Seria and return to Amendyr, the magical kingdom of her birth, she travels across the border in search of her grandmother to learn more about her visions. But before she can find her family, she is captured by a witch, rescued by a handsome stranger, and forced to join a strange group of forest-dwellers with even stranger magical abilities. With the help of her new lover, her new family, and her eccentric new teacher, she must learn to gain control of her powers and do some rescuing of her own before they take control of her instead.

The Witch's Daughter
ISBN: 978131672643
Ailynn Gothel has always been the perfect daughter. Thanks to her mother's teachings, she knows how to heal the sick, conjure the elements, and take care of Raisa, her closest and dearest friend. But when Ailynn's feelings for Raisa grow deeper, her simple life falls apart. Her mother hides Raisa deep in a cave to shield her from the world, and

Ailynn must leave home in search of a spell to free her. While the kingdom beyond the forest is full of dangers, Ailynn's greatest fear is that Raisa will no longer want her when she returns. She is a witch's daughter, after all—and witches never get their happily ever after.

Desert Palm Press

Written with Michelle Magly

Dark Horizons
ISBN: 9781310892646
Lieutenant Taylor Morgan has never met an ikthian that wasn't trying to kill her, but when she accidentally takes one of the aliens hostage, she finds herself with an entirely new set of responsibilities. Her captive, Maia Kalanis, is no normal ikthian, and the encroaching Dominion is willing to do just about anything to get her back. Her superiors want to use Maia as a bargaining chip, but the more time Taylor spends alone with her, the more conflicted she becomes. Torn between Maia and her duty to her home-world, Taylor must decide where her loyalties lie.

Starless Nights (Dark Horizons Book 2)
ISBN: 9781310317736
In this sequel to Dark Horizons Taylor and Maia did not know where they would go when they fled Earth. They trusted Akton to take them somewhere safe. Leaving behind a wake of chaos and disorder, Coalition soldier Rachel is left to deal with the backlash of Taylor's actions, and soon finds herself chasing after the runaways. Rachel quickly learns the final frontier is not a forgiving place for humans, but her chances for survival are better out there than back on Earth. Meanwhile, Taylor and Maia find themselves living off the generosity of rebel leader Sorra, an ikthian living a double life for the sake of the rebellion. With Maia's research in hand, Sorra believes they can deliver a fatal blow against the Dominion.

Desert Palm Press

All The Pretty Things (Revised Edition)
ISBN: 9781311061393
With the launch of her political campaign, the last thing Tess needed was a distraction. She had enough to deal with running as a Republican and a closeted lesbian. But when Special Agent Robin Hart from the FBI arrives in Cincinnati to investigate a corruption case, Tess finds herself spending more time than she should with the attractive woman. Things get a little more complicated when Robin begins to display signs of affection, and Tess fears her own outing might erupt in political scandal and sink all chances of pursuing her dreams.

Cover Design By : Rachel George
www.rachelgeorgeillustration.com

Note to Readers:

We have made every effort to edit this book. However, typos do slip in. If you find an error in the text, please email: lee@desertpalmpress.com so the issue can be corrected. We appreciate you as a reader and want to ensure you enjoy the reading process.

Bright blessing.

Desert Palm Press